PENGUIN BOOKS

THE PEARL
THE RED PONY

John Steinbeck was born in Salinas, California, in 1902. The town is a few miles from the Pacific Coast and near the fertile Salinas Valley—an area that was to be the background of much of his fiction. He studied marine biology at Stanford University but left without taking a degree and, after a series of laboring jobs, began to write. An attempt at a free-lance literary career in New York failed, and he returned to California, continuing to write in a lonely cottage. Popular success came to him only in 1935 with *Tortilla Flat*. That book's promise was confirmed by succeeding works—*In Dubious Battle*, *Of Mice and Men*, and especially *The Grapes of Wrath*, a novel so powerful that it remains among the archetypes of American culture. Often set in California, Steinbeck's later books include *Cannery Row*, *The Wayward Bus*, *East of Eden*, *The Short Reign of Pippin IV*, and *Travels with Charley*. He died in 1968, having won a Nobel Prize in 1962. In announcing the award, the Swedish Academy declared: ". . . he had no mind to be an unoffending comforter and entertainer. Instead, the topics he chose were serious and denunciatory, for instance the bitter strikes on California's fruit and cotton plantations. . . . His literary power steadily gained impetus. . . . The little masterpiece *Of Mice and Men* . . . was followed by those incomparable short stories which he collected together in the volume *The Long Valley*. The way had now been paved for the great work . . . the epic chronicle *The Grapes of Wrath*."

BY JOHN STEINBECK

FICTION

Cup of Gold

The Pastures of Heaven

To a God Unknown

Tortilla Flat

In Dubious Battle

Saint Katy the Virgin

Of Mice and Men

The Red Pony

The Long Valley

The Grapes of Wrath

The Moon Is Down

Cannery Row

The Wayward Bus

The Pearl

Burning Bright

(play in story form)

East of Eden

Sweet Thursday

The Winter of Our Discontent

The Short Reign of Pippin IV:

A Fabrication

NONFICTION

Sea of Cortez: *A Leisurely Journal of Travel and Research*

(in collaboration with Edward F. Ricketts)

Bombs Away: *The Story of a Bomber Team*

A Russian Journal *(with pictures by Robert Capa)*

The Log from the *Sea of Cortez*

Once There Was a War

Travels with Charley in Search of America

America and Americans

Journal of a Novel: *The* East of Eden *Letters*

PLAYS, A DOCUMENTARY, AND A SCREENPLAY

Of Mice and Men

The Moon Is Down

The Forgotten Village

Viva Zapata!

COLLECTIONS

The Portable Steinbeck

The Short Novels of John Steinbeck

Steinbeck: A Life In Letters

CRITICAL LIBRARY EDITION

The Grapes of Wrath *(edited by Peter Lisca)*

John Steinbeck

THE PEARL

Drawings by José Clemente Orozco

THE RED PONY

Illustrations by Wesley Dennis

PENGUIN BOOKS

Penguin Books Ltd, Harmondsworth,
Middlesex, England
Penguin Books, 625 Madison Avenue,
New York, New York 10022, U.S.A.
Penguin Books Australia Ltd, Ringwood,
Victoria, Australia
Penguin Books Canada Limited, 2801 John Street,
Markham, Ontario, Canada L3R 1B4
Penguin Books (N.Z.) Ltd, 182–190 Wairau Road,
Auckland 10, New Zealand

The Pearl published by The Viking Press 1947
The Red Pony published by The Viking Press 1945
Viking Compass Edition in one volume published 1965
Reprinted 1965, 1966, 1967, 1968 (twice),
1969, 1970, 1971, 1972, 1973 (twice), 1975
Published in Penguin Books 1976
Reprinted 1977, 1978, 1979, 1980 (twice), 1981 (twice)

ISBN 0 14 00.4232 6

Library of Congress catalog card number: 47–8597

Printed in the United States of America by
Offset Paperback Mfrs., Inc., Dallas, Pennsylvania
Set in Linotype Janson

Contents

The Pearl

IN THE town they tell the story of the great pearl—how it was found and how it was lost again. They tell of Kino, the fisherman, and of his wife, Juana, and of the baby, Coyotito. And because the story has been told so often, it has taken root in every man's mind. And, as with all retold tales that are in people's hearts, there are only good and bad things and black and white things and good and evil things and no in-between anywhere.

"If this story is a parable, perhaps everyone takes his own meaning from it and reads his own life into it. In any case, they say in the town that . . ."

KINO awakened in the near dark. The stars still shone and the day had drawn only a pale wash of light in the lower sky to the east. The roosters had been crowing for some time, and the early pigs were already beginning their ceaseless turning of twigs and bits of wood to see whether anything to eat had been overlooked. Outside the brush house in the tuna clump, a covey of little birds chittered and flurried with their wings.

Kino's eyes opened, and he looked first at the lightening square which was the door and then he looked at the hanging box where Coyotito slept. And last he turned his head to Juana, his wife, who lay beside him on the mat, her blue head shawl over her nose and over her breasts and around the small of her back. Juana's eyes were open too. Kino could never remember seeing them closed when he awakened. Her dark eyes made little reflected stars. She was looking at him as she was always looking at him when he awakened.

Kino heard the little splash of morning waves on the beach. It was very good—Kino closed his eyes again to listen to his music. Perhaps he alone did this and perhaps all of his people did it. His people had once been great makers of songs so that everything they saw or thought or did or heard became a song. That was very long ago. The songs remained; Kino knew them, but no new songs were added. That does not mean that there were no personal songs. In Kino's head there was a song now, clear and soft, and if he had been able to speak of it, he would have called it the Song of the Family.

His blanket was over his nose to protect him from the dank air. His eyes flicked to a rustle beside him. It was

Juana arising, almost soundlessly. On her hard bare feet she went to the hanging box where Coyotito slept, and she leaned over and said a little reassuring word. Coyotito looked up for a moment and closed his eyes and slept again.

Juana went to the fire pit and uncovered a coal and fanned it alive while she broke little pieces of brush over it.

Now Kino got up and wrapped his blanket about his head and nose and shoulders. He slipped his feet into his sandals and went outside to watch the dawn.

Outside the door he squatted down and gathered the blanket ends about his knees. He saw the specks of Gulf clouds flame high in the air. And a goat came near and sniffed at him and stared with its cold yellow eyes. Behind him Juana's fire leaped into flame and threw spears of light through the chinks of the brush-house wall and threw a wavering square of light out the door. A late moth blustered in to find the fire. The Song of the Family came now from behind Kino. And the rhythm of the family song was the grinding stone where Juana worked the corn for the morning cakes.

The dawn came quickly now, a wash, a glow, a lightness, and then an explosion of fire as the sun arose out of the Gulf. Kino looked down to cover his eyes from the glare. He could hear the pat of the corn-cakes in the house and the rich smell of them on the cooking plate. The ants were busy on the ground, big black ones with shiny bodies, and little dusty quick ants. Kino watched with the detachment of God while a dusty ant frantically tried to escape the sand trap an ant lion had dug for him. A thin, timid dog came close and, at a soft word from Kino, curled up, arranged its tail neatly over its feet, and laid its chin delicately on the pile. It was a black dog with yellow-gold spots where its eyebrows should have been. It was a morning like other mornings and yet perfect among mornings.

Kino heard the creak of the rope when Juana took Coyotito out of his hanging box and cleaned him and hammocked him in her shawl in a loop that placed him close to her breast. Kino could see these things without looking at them. Juana sang softly an ancient song that had only three notes and yet endless variety of interval. And this was part of the family song too. It was all part. Sometimes it rose to an aching chord that caught the throat, saying this is safety, this is warmth, this is the *Whole*.

Across the brush fence were other brush houses, and the smoke came from them too, and the sound of breakfast, but those were other songs, their pigs were other pigs, their wives were not Juana. Kino was young and strong and his black hair hung over his brown forehead. His eyes were warm and fierce and bright and his mustache was thin and coarse. He lowered his blanket from his nose now, for the dark poisonous air was gone and the yellow sunlight fell on the house. Near the brush fence two roosters bowed and feinted at each other with squared wings and neck feathers ruffled out. It would be a clumsy fight. They were not game chickens. Kino watched them for a moment, and then his eyes went up to a flight of wild doves twinkling inland to the hills. The world was awake now, and Kino arose and went into his brush house.

As he came through the door Juana stood up from the glowing fire pit. She put Coyotito back in his hanging box and then she combed her black hair and braided it in two braids and tied the ends with thin green ribbon. Kino squatted by the fire pit and rolled a hot corncake and dipped it in sauce and ate it. And he drank a little pulque and that was breakfast. That was the only breakfast he had ever known outside of feast days and one incredible fiesta on cookies that had nearly killed him. When Kino had finished, Juana came back to the fire and ate her breakfast. They had spoken once, but there is not need for speech if

it is only a habit anyway. Kino sighed with satisfaction—
and that was conversation.

The sun was warming the brush house, breaking through
its crevices in long streaks. And one of the streaks fell on
the hanging box where Coyotito lay, and on the ropes that
held it.

It was a tiny movement that drew their eyes to the hanging box. Kino and Juana froze in their positions. Down the
rope that hung the baby's box from the roof support a
scorpion moved slowly. His stinging tail was straight out
behind him, but he could whip it up in a flash of time.

Kino's breath whistled in his nostrils and he opened his
mouth to stop it. And then the startled look was gone from
him and the rigidity from his body. In his mind a new song
had come, the Song of Evil, the music of the enemy, of any
foe of the family, a savage, secret, dangerous melody, and
underneath, the Song of the Family cried plaintively.

The scorpion moved delicately down the rope toward
the box. Under her breath Juana repeated an ancient magic
to guard against such evil, and on top of that she muttered
a Hail Mary between clenched teeth. But Kino was in motion. His body glided quietly across the room, noiselessly
and smoothly. His hands were in front of him, palms down,
and his eyes were on the scorpion. Beneath it in the hanging box Coyotito laughed and reached up his hand toward
it. It sensed danger when Kino was almost within reach of
it. It stopped, and its tail rose up over its back in little jerks
and the curved thorn on the tail's end glistened.

Kino stood perfectly still. He could hear Juana whispering the old magic again, and he could hear the evil music of
the enemy. He could not move until the scorpion moved,
and it felt for the source of the death that was coming to it.
Kino's hand went forward very slowly, very smoothly. The
thorned tail jerked upright. And at that moment the laugh-
ing Coyotito shook the rope and the scorpion fell.

Kino's hand leaped to catch it, but it fell past his fingers, fell on the baby's shoulder, landed and struck. Then, snarling, Kino had it, had it in his fingers, rubbing it to a paste in his hands. He threw it down and beat it into the earth floor with his fist, and Coyotito screamed with pain in his box. But Kino beat and stamped the enemy until it was only a fragment and a moist place in the dirt. His teeth were bared and fury flared in his eyes and the Song of the Enemy roared in his ears.

But Juana had the baby in her arms now. She found the puncture with redness starting from it already. She put her lips down over the puncture and sucked hard and spat and sucked again while Coyotito screamed.

Kino hovered; he was helpless, he was in the way.

The screams of the baby brought the neighbors. Out of their brush houses they poured—Kino's brother Juan Tomás and his fat wife Apolonia and their four children crowded in the door and blocked the entrance, while behind them others tried to look in, and one small boy crawled among legs to have a look. And those in front passed the word back to those behind—"Scorpion. The baby has been stung."

Juana stopped sucking the puncture for a moment. The little hole was slightly enlarged and its edges whitened from the sucking, but the red swelling extended farther around it in a hard lymphatic mound. And all of these people knew about the scorpion. An adult might be very ill from the sting, but a baby could easily die from the poison. First, they knew, would come swelling and fever and tightened throat, and then cramps in the stomach, and then Coyotito might die if enough of the poison had gone in. But the stinging pain of the bite was going away. Coyotito's screams turned to moans.

Kino had wondered often at the iron in his patient, fragile wife. She, who was obedient and respectful and cheerful and patient, she could arch her back in child pain with hardly a cry. She could stand fatigue and hunger almost better than Kino himself. In the canoe she was like a strong man. And now she did a most surprising thing.

"The doctor," she said. "Go to get the doctor."

The word was passed out among the neighbors where they stood close packed in the little yard behind the brush fence. And they repeated among themselves, "Juana wants the doctor." A wonderful thing, a memorable thing, to want the doctor. To get him would be a remarkable thing. The doctor never came to the cluster of brush houses. Why should he, when he had more than he could do to take care of the rich people who lived in the stone and plaster houses of the town.

"He would not come," the people in the yard said.

"He would not come," the people in the door said, and the thought got into Kino.

"The doctor would not come," Kino said to Juana.

She looked up at him, her eyes as cold as the eyes of a lioness. This was Juana's first baby—this was nearly everything there was in Juana's world. And Kino saw her determination and the music of the family sounded in his head with a steely tone.

"Then we will go to him," Juana said, and with one hand she arranged her dark blue shawl over her head and made of one end of it a sling to hold the moaning baby and made of the other end of it a shade over his eyes to protect him from the light. The people in the door pushed against those behind to let her through. Kino followed her. They went out of the gate to the rutted path and the neighbors followed them.

The thing had become a neighborhood affair. They made a quick soft-footed procession into the center of the town, first Juana and Kino, and behind them Juan Tomás and Apolonia, her big stomach jiggling with the strenuous pace, then all the neighbors with the children trotting on the flanks. And the yellow sun threw their black shadows ahead of them so that they walked on their own shadows.

They came to the place where the brush houses stopped and the city of stone and plaster began, the city of harsh outer walls and inner cool gardens where a little water played and the bougainvillaea crusted the walls with purple and brick-red and white. They heard from the secret gardens the singing of caged birds and heard the splash of cooling water on hot flagstones. The procession crossed the blinding plaza and passed in front of the church. It had grown now, and on the outskirts the hurrying newcomers were being softly informed how the baby had been stung by a scorpion, how the father and mother were taking it to the doctor.

And the newcomers, particularly the beggars from the front of the church who were great experts in financial analysis, looked quickly at Juana's old blue skirt, saw the tears in her shawl, appraised the green ribbon on her braids, read the age of Kino's blanket and the thousand washings of his clothes, and set them down as poverty people and went along to see what kind of drama might develop. The four beggars in front of the church knew everything in the town. They were students of the expressions of young women as they went in to confession, and they saw them as they came out and read the nature of the sin. They knew every little scandal and some very big crimes. They slept at their posts in the shadow of the church so that no one crept in for consolation without their knowledge. And they knew the doctor. They knew his ignorance, his cruelty, his avarice, his appetites, his sins. They knew his clumsy abortions and the little brown pennies he gave sparingly for alms. They had seen his corpses go into the church. And, since early Mass was over and business was slow, they followed the procession, these endless searchers after perfect knowledge of their fellow men, to see what the fat lazy doctor would do about an indigent baby with a scorpion bite.

The scurrying procession came at last to the big gate in the wall of the doctor's house. They could hear the splashing water and the singing of caged birds and the sweep of the long brooms on the flagstones. And they could smell the frying of good bacon from the doctor's house.

Kino hesitated a moment. This doctor was not of his people. This doctor was of a race which for nearly four hundred years had beaten and starved and robbed and despised Kino's race, and frightened it too, so that the indigene came humbly to the door. And as always when he came near to one of this race, Kino felt weak and afraid and angry at the same time. Rage and terror went together. He could kill the doctor more easily than he could talk to him, for all of the doctor's race spoke to all of Kino's race as though they were simple animals. And as Kino raised his right hand to the iron ring knocker in the gate, rage swelled in him, and the pounding music of the enemy beat in his ears, and his lips drew tight against his teeth—but with his left hand he reached to take off his hat. The iron ring pounded against the gate. Kino took off his hat and stood waiting. Coyotito moaned a little in Juana's arms, and she spoke softly to him. The procession crowded close, the better to see and hear.

After a moment the big gate opened a few inches. Kino could see the green coolness of the garden and little splashing fountain through the opening. The man who looked out at him was one of his own race. Kino spoke to him in the old language. "The little one—the first born—has been poisoned by the scorpion," Kino said. "He requires the skill of the healer."

The gate closed a little, and the servant refused to speak in the old language. "A little moment," he said. "I go to inform myself," and he closed the gate and slid the bolt home. The glaring sun threw the bunched shadows of the people blackly on the white wall.

In his chamber the doctor sat up in his high bed. He had on his dressing gown of red watered silk that had come from Paris, a little tight over the chest now if it was buttoned. On his lap was a silver tray with a silver chocolate pot and a tiny cup of eggshell china, so delicate that it looked silly when he lifted it with his big hand, lifted it with the tips of thumb and forefinger and spread the other three fingers wide to get them out of the way. His eyes rested in puffy little hammocks of flesh and his mouth drooped with discontent. He was growing very stout, and his voice was hoarse with the fat that pressed on his throat. Beside him on a table was a small oriental gong and a bowl of cigarettes. The furnishings of the room were heavy and dark and gloomy. The pictures were religious, even the large tinted photograph of his dead wife, who, if Masses willed and paid for out of her own estate could do it, was in Heaven. The doctor had once for a short time been a part of the great world and his whole subsequent life was memory and longing for France. "That," he said, "was civilized living" —by which he meant that on a small income he had been able to keep a mistress and eat in restaurants. He poured his second cup of chocolate and crumbled a sweet biscuit in his fingers. The servant from the gate came to the open door and stood waiting to be noticed.

"Yes?" the doctor asked.

"It is a little Indian with a baby. He says a scorpion stung it."

The doctor put his cup down gently before he let his anger rise.

"Have I nothing better to do than cure insect bites for 'little Indians'? I am a doctor, not a veterinary."

"Yes, Patron," said the servant.

"Has he any money?" the doctor demanded. "No, they never have any money. I, I alone in the world am supposed to work for nothing—and I am tired of it. See if he has any money!"

At the gate the servant opened the door a trifle and looked out at the waiting people. And this time he spoke in the old language.

"Have you money to pay for the treatment?"

Now Kino reached into a secret place somewhere under his blanket. He brought out a paper folded many times. Crease by crease he unfolded it, until at last there came to view eight small misshapen seed pearls, as ugly and gray as little ulcers, flattened and almost valueless. The servant took the paper and closed the gate again, but this time he was not gone long. He opened the gate just wide enough to pass the paper back.

"The doctor has gone out," he said. "He was called to a serious case." And he shut the gate quickly out of shame.

And now a wave of shame went over the whole procession. They melted away. The beggars went back to the church steps, the stragglers moved off, and the neighbors departed so that the public shaming of Kino would not be in their eyes.

For a long time Kino stood in front of the gate with Juana beside him. Slowly he put his suppliant hat on his head. Then, without warning, he struck the gate a crushing blow with his fist. He looked down in wonder at his split knuckles and at the blood that flowed down between his fingers.

THE town lay on a broad estuary, its old yellow plastered buildings hugging the beach. And on the beach the white and blue canoes that came from Nayarit were drawn up, canoes preserved for generations by a hard shell-like waterproof plaster whose making was a secret of the fishing people. They were high and graceful canoes with curving bow and stern and a braced section midships where a mast could be stepped to carry a small lateen sail.

The beach was yellow sand, but at the water's edge a rubble of shell and algae took its place. Fiddler crabs bubbled and sputtered in their holes in the sand, and in the shallows little lobsters popped in and out of their tiny homes in the rubble and sand. The sea bottom was rich with crawling and swimming and growing things. The brown algae waved in the gentle currents and the green eel grass swayed and little sea horses clung to its stems. Spotted botete, the poison fish, lay on the bottom in the eel-grass beds, and the bright-colored swimming crabs scampered over them.

On the beach the hungry dogs and the hungry pigs of the town searched endlessly for any dead fish or sea bird that might have floated in on a rising tide.

Although the morning was young, the hazy mirage was up. The uncertain air that magnified some things and blotted out others hung over the whole Gulf so that all sights were unreal and vision could not be trusted; so that sea and land had the sharp clarities and the vagueness of a dream. Thus it might be that the people of the Gulf trust things of the spirit and things of the imagination, but they do not trust their eyes to show them distance or clear outline or any optical exactness. Across the estuary from the town one section of mangroves stood clear and telescopically defined, while another mangrove clump was a hazy black-green blob. Part of the far shore disappeared into a shimmer that looked like water. There was no certainty in seeing, no proof that what you saw was there or was not there. And the people of the Gulf expected all places were that way, and it was not strange to them. A copper haze hung over the water, and the hot morning sun beat on it and made it vibrate blindingly.

The brush houses of the fishing people were back from the beach on the right-hand side of the town, and the canoes were drawn up in front of this area.

Kino and Juana came slowly down to the beach and to Kino's canoe, which was the one thing of value he owned in the world. It was very old. Kino's grandfather had brought it from Nayarit, and he had given it to Kino's father, and so it had come to Kino. It was at once property and source of food, for a man with a boat can guarantee a woman that she will eat something. It is the bulwark against starvation. And every year Kino refinished his canoe with the hard shell-like plaster by the secret method that had also come to him from his father. Now he came to the canoe and touched the bow tenderly as he always did. He laid his diving rock and his basket and the two ropes in the sand by the canoe. And he folded his blanket and laid it in the bow.

Juana laid Coyotito on the blanket, and she placed her shawl over him so that the hot sun could not shine on him. He was quiet now, but the swelling on his shoulder had continued up his neck and under his ear and his face was puffed and feverish. Juana went to the water and waded in. She gathered some brown seaweed and made a flat damp poultice of it, and this she applied to the baby's swollen shoulder, which was as good a remedy as any and probably better than the doctor could have done. But the remedy lacked his authority because it was simple and didn't cost anything. The stomach cramps had not come to Coyotito.

Perhaps Juana had sucked out the poison in time, but she had not sucked out her worry over her first-born. She had not prayed directly for the recovery of the baby—she had prayed that they might find a pearl with which to hire the doctor to cure the baby, for the minds of people are as unsubstantial as the mirage of the Gulf.

Now Kino and Juana slid the canoe down the beach to the water, and when the bow floated, Juana climbed in, while Kino pushed the stern in and waded beside it until it floated lightly and trembled on the little breaking waves. Then in co-ordination Juana and Kino drove their double-bladed paddles into the sea, and the canoe creased the water and hissed with speed. The other pearlers were gone out long since. In a few moments Kino could see them clustered in the haze, riding over the oyster bed.

Light filtered down through the water to the bed where the frilly pearl oysters lay fastened to the rubbly bottom, a bottom strewn with shells of broken, opened oysters. This was the bed that had raised the King of Spain to be a great power in Europe in past years, had helped to pay for his wars, and had decorated the churches for his soul's sake. The gray oysters with ruffles like skirts on the shells, the barnacle-crusted oysters with little bits of weed clinging to the skirts and small crabs climbing over them. An accident could happen to these oysters, a grain of sand could lie in the folds of muscle and irritate the flesh until in self-protection the flesh coated the grain with a layer of smooth cement. But once started, the flesh continued to coat the foreign body until it fell free in some tidal flurry or until the oyster was destroyed. For centuries men had dived down and torn the oysters from the beds and ripped them open, looking for the coated grains of sand. Swarms of fish lived near the bed to live near the oysters thrown back by the searching men and to nibble at the shining inner shells. But the pearls were accidents, and the finding of one was luck, a little pat on the back by God or the gods or both.

Kino had two ropes, one tied to a heavy stone and one to a basket. He stripped off his shirt and trousers and laid his hat in the bottom of the canoe. The water was oily smooth. He took his rock in one hand and his basket in the other, and he slipped feet first over the side and the rock carried him to the bottom. The bubbles rose behind him until the water cleared and he could see. Above, the surface of the water was an undulating mirror of brightness, and he could see the bottoms of the canoes sticking through it.

Kino moved cautiously so that the water would not be obscured with mud or sand. He hooked his foot in the loop on his rock and his hands worked quickly, tearing the oysters loose, some singly, others in clusters. He laid them in his basket. In some places the oysters clung to one another so that they came free in lumps.

Now, Kino's people had sung of everything that happened or existed. They had made songs to the fishes, to the sea in anger and to the sea in calm, to the light and the dark and the sun and the moon, and the songs were all in Kino and in his people—every song that had ever been made, even the ones forgotten. And as he filled his basket the song was in Kino, and the beat of the song was his pounding heart as it ate the oxygen from his held breath, and the melody of the song was the gray-green water and the little scuttling animals and the clouds of fish that flitted by and were gone. But in the song there was a secret little inner song, hardly perceptible, but always there, sweet and secret and clinging, almost hiding in the counter-melody, and this was the Song of the Pearl That Might Be, for every shell thrown in the basket might contain a pearl. Chance was against it, but luck and the gods might be for it. And in the canoe above him Kino knew that Juana was making the magic of prayer, her face set rigid and her muscles hard to force the luck, to tear the luck out of the gods' hands, for she needed the luck for the swollen shoulder of Coyotito. And because the need was great and the desire was great, the little secret melody of the pearl that might be was stronger this morning. Whole phrases of it came clearly and softly into the Song of the Undersea.

Kino, in his pride and youth and strength, could remain down over two minutes without strain, so that he worked deliberately, selecting the largest shells. Because they were disturbed, the oyster shells were tightly closed. A little to his right a hummock of rubbly rock stuck up, covered with young oysters not ready to take. Kino moved next to the hummock, and then, beside it, under a little overhang, he saw a very large oyster lying by itself, not covered with its clinging brothers. The shell was partly open, for the overhang protected this ancient oyster, and in the lip-like muscle Kino saw a ghostly gleam, and then the shell closed down. His heart beat out a heavy rhythm and the melody of the maybe pearl shrilled in his ears. Slowly he forced the oyster loose and held it tightly against his breast. He kicked his foot free from the rock loop, and his body rose to the surface and his black hair gleamed in the sunlight. He reached over the side of the canoe and laid the oyster in the bottom.

Then Juana steadied the boat while he climbed in. His eyes were shining with excitement, but in decency he pulled up his rock, and then he pulled up his basket of oysters and lifted them in. Juana sensed his excitement, and she pretended to look away. It is not good to want a thing too much. It sometimes drives the luck away. You must want it just enough, and you must be very tactful with God or the gods. But Juana stopped breathing. Very deliberately Kino opened his short strong knife. He looked speculatively at the basket. Perhaps it would be better to open *the* oyster last. He took a small oyster from the basket, cut the muscle, searched the folds of flesh, and threw it in the water. Then

he seemed to see the great oyster for the first time. He squatted in the bottom of the canoe, picked up the shell and examined it. The flutes were shining black to brown, and only a few small barnacles adhered to the shell. Now Kino was reluctant to open it. What he had seen, he knew, might be a reflection, a piece of flat shell accidently drifted in or a complete illusion. In this Gulf of uncertain light there were more illusions than realities.

But Juana's eyes were on him and she could not wait. She put her hand on Coyotito's covered head. "Open it," she said softly.

Kino deftly slipped his knife into the edge of the shell. Through the knife he could feel the muscle tighten hard. He worked the blade lever-wise and the closing muscle parted and the shell fell apart. The lip-like flesh writhed up and then subsided. Kino lifted the flesh, and there it lay, the great pearl, perfect as the moon. It captured the light and refined it and gave it back in silver incandescence. It was as large as a sea-gull's egg. It was the greatest pearl in the world.

Juana caught her breath and moaned a little. And to Kino the secret melody of the maybe pearl broke clear and beautiful, rich and warm and lovely, glowing and gloating and triumphant. In the surface of the great pearl he could see dream forms. He picked the pearl from the dying flesh and held it in his palm, and he turned it over and saw that its curve was perfect. Juana came near to stare at it in his hand, and it was the hand he had smashed against the doctor's gate, and the torn flesh of the knuckles was turned grayish white by the sea water.

Instinctively Juana went to Coyotito where he lay on his father's blanket. She lifted the poultice of seaweed and looked at the shoulder. "Kino," she cried shrilly.

He looked past his pearl, and he saw that the swelling was going out of the baby's shoulder, the poison was receding from its body. Then Kino's fist closed over the pearl and his emotion broke over him. He put back his head and howled. His eyes rolled up and he screamed and his body was rigid. The men in the other canoes looked up, startled, and then they dug their paddles into the sea and raced toward Kino's canoe.

A TOWN is a thing like a colonial animal. A town has a nervous system and a head and shoulders and feet. A town is a thing separate from all other towns, so that there are no two towns alike. And a town has a whole emotion. How news travels through a town is a mystery not easily to be solved. News seems to move faster than small boys can scramble and dart to tell it, faster than women can call it over the fences.

Before Kino and Juana and the other fishers had come to Kino's brush house, the nerves of the town were pulsing and vibrating with the news—Kino had found the Pearl of the World. Before panting little boys could strangle out the words, their mothers knew it. The news swept on past the brush houses, and it washed in a foaming wave into the town of stone and plaster. It came to the priest walking in his garden, and it put a thoughtful look in his eyes and a memory of certain repairs necessary to the church. He wondered what the pearl would be worth. And he wondered whether he had baptized Kino's baby, or married him for that matter. The news came to the shopkeepers, and they looked at men's clothes that had not sold so well.

The news came to the doctor where he sat with a woman whose illness was age, though neither she nor the doctor would admit it. And when it was made plain who Kino was, the doctor grew stern and judicious at the same time. "He is a client of mine," the doctor said. "I am treating his child for a scorpion sting." And the doctor's eyes rolled up a little in their fat hammocks and he thought of Paris. He remembered the room he had lived in there as a great and luxurious place, and he remembered the hard-faced woman who had lived with him as a beautiful and kind girl, although she had been none of these three. The doctor looked past his aged patient and saw himself sitting in a restaurant in Paris and a waiter was just opening a bottle of wine.

The news came early to the beggars in front of the church, and it made them giggle a little with pleasure, for they knew that there is no almsgiver in the world like a poor man who is suddenly lucky.

Kino has found the Pearl of the World. In the town, in little offices, sat the men who bought pearls from the fishers. They waited in their chairs until the pearls came in, and then they cackled and fought and shouted and threatened until they reached the lowest price the fisherman would stand. But there was a price below which they dared not go, for it had happened that a fisherman in despair had given his pearls to the church. And when the buying was over, these buyers sat alone and their fingers played restlessly with the pearls, and they wished they owned the pearls. For there were not many buyers really—there was only one, and he kept these agents in separate offices to give a semblance of competition. The news came to these men, and their eyes squinted and their fingertips burned a little, and each one thought how the patron could not live forever and someone had to take his place. And each one thought how with some capital he could get a new start.

All manner of people grew interested in Kino—people with things to sell and people with favors to ask. Kino had found the Pearl of the World. The essence of pearl mixed with essence of men and a curious dark residue was precipitated. Every man suddenly became related to Kino's pearl, and Kino's pearl went into the dreams, the speculations, the schemes, the plans, the futures, the wishes, the needs, the lusts, the hungers, of everyone, and only one person stood in the way and that was Kino, so that he became curiously every man's enemy. The news stirred up something infinitely black and evil in the town; the black distillate was like the scorpion, or like hunger in the smell of food, or like loneliness when love is withheld. The poison sacs of the town began to manufacture venom, and the town swelled and puffed with the pressure of it.

But Kino and Juana did not know these things. Because they were happy and excited they thought everyone shared their joy. Juan Tomás and Apolonia did, and they were the world too. In the afternoon, when the sun had gone over the mountains of the Peninsula to sink in the outward sea, Kino squatted in his house with Juana beside him. And the brush house was crowded with neighbors. Kino held the great pearl in his hand, and it was warm and alive in his hand. And the music of the pearl had merged with the music of the family so that one beautified the other. The neighbors looked at the pearl in Kino's hand and they wondered how such luck could come to any man.

And Juan Tomás, who squatted on Kino's right hand because he was his brother, asked, "What will you do now that you have become a rich man?"

Kino looked into his pearl, and Juana cast her eyelashes down and arranged her shawl to cover her face so that her excitement could not be seen. And in the incandescence of the pearl the pictures formed of the things Kino's mind had considered in the past and had given up as impossible. In the pearl he saw Juana and Coyotito and himself standing and kneeling at the high altar, and they were being married now that they could pay. He spoke softly, "We will be married—in the church."

In the pearl he saw how they were dressed—Juana in a shawl stiff with newness and a new skirt, and from under the long skirt Kino could see that she wore shoes. It was in the pearl—the picture glowing there. He himself was dressed in new white clothes, and he carried a new hat—not of straw but of fine black felt—and he too wore shoes—not sandals but shoes that laced. But Coyotito—he was the one

—he wore a blue sailor suit from the United States and a little yachting cap such as Kino had seen once when a pleasure boat put into the estuary. All of these things Kino saw in the lucent pearl and he said, "We will have new clothes."

And the music of the pearl rose like a chorus of trumpets in his ears.

Then to the lovely gray surface of the pearl came the little things Kino wanted: a harpoon to take the place of one lost a year ago, a new harpoon of iron with a ring in the end of the shaft; and—his mind could hardly make the leap —a rifle—but why not, since he was so rich. And Kino saw Kino in the pearl; Kino holding a Winchester carbine. It was the wildest daydreaming and very pleasant. His lips moved hesitantly over this—"A rifle," he said. "Perhaps a rifle."

It was the rifle that broke down the barriers. This was an impossibility, and if he could think of having a rifle whole horizons were burst and he could rush on. For it is said that humans are never satisfied, that you give them one thing and they want something more. And this is said in disparagement, whereas it is one of the greatest talents the species has and one that has made it superior to animals that are satisfied with what they have.

The neighbors, close pressed and silent in the house, nodded their heads at his wild imaginings. And a man in the rear murmured, "A rifle. He will have a rifle."

But the music of the pearl was shrilling with triumph in Kino. Juana looked up, and her eyes were wide at Kino's courage and at his imagination. And electric strength had come to him now the horizons were kicked out. In the pearl he saw Coyotito sitting at a little desk in a school, just as Kino had once seen it through an open door. And Coyotito was dressed in a jacket, and he had on a white collar and a broad silken tie. Moreover, Coyotito was writing on a big piece of paper. Kino looked at his neighbors fiercely.

"My son will go to school," he said, and the neighbors were hushed. Juana caught her breath sharply. Her eyes were bright as she watched him, and she looked quickly down at Coyotito in her arms to see whether this might be possible.

But Kino's face shone with prophecy. "My son will read and open the books, and my son will write and will know writing. And my son will make numbers, and these things will make us free because he will know—he will know and through him we will know." And in the pearl Kino saw himself and Juana squatting by the little fire in the brush hut while Coyotito read from a great book. "This is what the pearl will do," said Kino. And he had never said so many words together in his life. And suddenly he was afraid of his talking. His hand closed down over the pearl and cut the light away from it. Kino was afraid as a man is afraid who says, "I will," without knowing.

Now the neighbors knew they had witnessed a great marvel. They knew that time would now date from Kino's pearl, and that they would discuss this moment for many years to come. If these things came to pass, they would recount how Kino looked and what he said and how his eyes shone, and they would say, "He was a man transfigured. Some power was given to him, and there it started. You see what a great man he has become, starting from that moment. And I myself saw it."

And if Kino's planning came to nothing, those same neighbors would say, "There it started. A foolish madness came over him so that he spoke foolish words. God keep us from such things. Yes, God punished Kino because he rebelled against the way things are. You see what has become of him. And I myself saw the moment when his reason left him."

Kino looked down at his closed hand and the knuckles were scabbed over and tight where he had struck the gate.

Now the dusk was coming. And Juana looped her shawl

under the baby so that he hung against her hip, and she went to the fire hole and dug a coal from the ashes and broke a few twigs over it and fanned a flame alive. The little flames danced on the faces of the neighbors. They knew they should go to their own dinners, but they were reluctant to leave.

The dark was almost in, and Juana's fire threw shadows on the brush walls when the whisper came in, passed from mouth to mouth. "The Father is coming—the priest is coming." The men uncovered their heads and stepped back from the door, and the women gathered their shawls about their faces and cast down their eyes. Kino and Juan Tomás, his brother, stood up. The priest came in—a graying, aging man with an old skin and a young sharp eye. Children, he considered these people, and he treated them like children.

"Kino," he said softly, "thou art named after a great man —and a great Father of the Church." He made it sound like a benediction. "Thy namesake tamed the desert and sweetened the minds of thy people, didst thou know that? It is in the books."

Kino looked quickly down at Coyotito's head, where he hung on Juana's hip. Some day, his mind said, that boy would know what things were in the books and what things were not. The music had gone out of Kino's head, but now, thinly, slowly, the melody of the morning, the music of evil, of the enemy sounded, but it was faint and weak. And Kino looked at his neighbors to see who might have brought this song in.

But the priest was speaking again. "It has come to me that thou hast found a great fortune, a great pearl."

Kino opened his hand and held it out, and the priest gasped a little at the size and beauty of the pearl. And then he said, "I hope thou wilt remember to give thanks, my son, to Him who has given thee this treasure, and to pray for guidance in the future."

Kino nodded dumbly, and it was Juana who spoke softly. "We will, Father. And we will be married now. Kino has said so." She looked at the neighbors for confirmation, and they nodded their heads solemnly.

The priest said, "It is pleasant to see that your first thoughts are good thoughts. God bless you, my children." He turned and left quietly, and the people let him through.

But Kino's hand had closed tightly on the pearl again, and he was glancing about suspiciously, for the evil song was in his ears, shrilling against the music of the pearl.

The neighbors slipped away to go to their houses, and Juana squatted by the fire and set her clay pot of boiled beans over the little flame. Kino stepped to the doorway and looked out. As always, he could smell the smoke from many fires, and he could see the hazy stars and feel the damp of the night air so that he covered his nose from it. The thin dog came to him and threshed itself in greeting like a wind-blown flag, and Kino looked down at it and didn't see it. He had broken through the horizons into a cold and lonely outside. He felt alone and unprotected, and scraping crickets and shrilling tree frogs and croaking toads seemed to be carrying the melody of evil. Kino shivered a little and drew his blanket more tightly against his nose. He carried the pearl still in his hand, tightly closed in his palm, and it was warm and smooth against his skin.

Behind him he heard Juana patting the cakes before she put them down on the clay cooking sheet. Kino felt all the warmth and security of his family behind him, and the Song of the Family came from behind him like the purring of a kitten. But now, by saying what his future was going to be like, he had created it. A plan is a real thing, and things projected are experienced. A plan once made and visualized becomes a reality along with other realities—never to be destroyed but easily to be attacked. Thus Kino's future was real, but having set it up, other forces were set up to destroy it, and this he knew, so that he had to prepare to meet the attack. And this Kino knew also—that the gods do not love men's plans, and the gods do not love success unless it comes by accident. He knew that the gods take their revenge on a man if he be successful through his own efforts. Consequently Kino was afraid of plans, but having made one, he could never destroy it. And to meet the attack, Kino was already making a hard skin for himself against the world. His eyes and his mind probed for danger before it appeared.

Standing in the door, he saw two men approach; and one of them carried a lantern which lighted the ground and the legs of the men. They turned in through the opening of Kino's brush fence and came to his door. And Kino saw that one was the doctor and the other the servant who had opened the gate in the morning. The split knuckles on Kino's right hand burned when he saw who they were.

The doctor said, "I was not in when you came this morning. But now, at the first chance, I have come to see the baby."

Kino stood in the door, filling it, and hatred raged and flamed in back of his eyes, and fear too, for the hundreds of years of subjugation were cut deep in him.

"The baby is nearly well now," he said curtly.

The doctor smiled, but his eyes in their little lymph-lined hammocks did not smile.

He said, "Sometimes, my friend, the scorpion sting has a curious effect. There will be apparent improvement, and then without warning—pouf!" He pursed his lips and made a little explosion to show how quick it could be, and he shifted his small black doctor's bag about so that the light of the lamp fell upon it, for he knew that Kino's race love the tools of any craft and trust them. "Sometimes," the doc-

tor went on in a liquid tone, "sometimes there will be a
withered leg or a blind eye or a crumpled back. Oh, I know
the sting of the scorpion, my friend, and I can cure it."

Kino felt the rage and hatred melting toward fear. He did
not know, and perhaps this doctor did. And he could not
take the chance of putting his certain ignorance against this
man's possible knowledge. He was trapped as his people
were always trapped, and would be until, as he had said,
they could be sure that the things in the books were really
in the books. He could not take a chance—not with the life
or with the straightness of Coyotito. He stood aside and let
the doctor and his man enter the brush hut.

Juana stood up from the fire and backed away as he entered, and she covered the baby's face with the fringe of her
shawl. And when the doctor went to her and held out his
hand, she clutched the baby tight and looked at Kino where
he stood with the fire shadows leaping on his face.

Kino nodded, and only then did she let the doctor take
the baby.

"Hold the light," the doctor said, and when the servant
held the lantern high, the doctor looked for a moment at
the wound on the baby's shoulder. He was thoughtful for a
moment and then he rolled back the baby's eyelid and
looked at the eyeball. He nodded his head while Coyotito
struggled against him.

"It is as I thought," he said. "The poison has gone inward
and it will strike soon. Come look!" He held the eyelid
down. "See—it is blue." And Kino, looking anxiously, saw
that indeed it was a little blue. And he didn't know whether
or not it was always a little blue. But the trap was set. He
couldn't take the chance.

The doctor's eyes watered in their little hammocks. "I
will give him something to try to turn the poison aside," he
said. And he handed the baby to Kino.

Then from his bag he took a little bottle of white powder

and a capsule of gelatine. He filled the capsule with the powder and closed it, and then around the first capsule he fitted a second capsule and closed it. Then he worked very deftly. He took the baby and pinched its lower lip until it opened its mouth. His fat fingers placed the capsule far back on the baby's tongue, back of the point where he could spit it out, and then from the floor he picked up the little pitcher of pulque and gave Coyotito a drink, and it was done. He looked again at the baby's eyeball and he pursed his lips and seemed to think.

At last he handed the baby back to Juana, and he turned to Kino. "I think the poison will attack within the hour," he said. "The medicine may save the baby from hurt, but I will come back in an hour. Perhaps I am in time to save him." He took a deep breath and went out of the hut, and his servant followed him with the lantern.

Now Juana had the baby under her shawl, and she stared at it with anxiety and fear. Kino came to her, and he lifted the shawl and stared at the baby. He moved his hand to look under the eyelid, and only then saw that the pearl was still in his hand. Then he went to a box by the wall, and from it he brought a piece of rag. He wrapped the pearl in the rag, then went to the corner of the brush house and dug a little hole with his fingers in the dirt floor, and he put the pearl in the hole and covered it up and concealed the place. And then he went to the fire where Juana was squatting, watching the baby's face.

The doctor, back in his house, settled into his chair and looked at his watch. His people brought him a little supper of chocolate and sweet cakes and fruit, and he stared at the food discontentedly.

In the houses of the neighbors the subject that would lead all conversations for a long time to come was aired for the first time to see how it would go. The neighbors showed one another with their thumbs how big the pearl was, and they made little caressing gestures to show how lovely it was. From now on they would watch Kino and Juana very closely to see whether riches turned their heads, as riches turn all people's heads. Everyone knew why the doctor had come. He was not good at dissembling and he was very well understood.

Out in the estuary a tight woven school of small fishes glittered and broke water to escape a school of great fishes that drove in to eat them. And in the houses the people could hear the swish of the small ones and the bouncing splash of the great ones as the slaughter went on. The dampness arose out of the Gulf and was deposited on bushes and cacti and on little trees in salty drops. And the night mice crept about on the ground and the little night hawks hunted them silently.

The skinny black puppy with flame spots over his eyes came to Kino's door and looked in. He nearly shook his hind quarters loose when Kino glanced up at him, and he subsided when Kino looked away. The puppy did not enter the house, but he watched with frantic interest while Kino ate his beans from the little pottery dish and wiped it clean with a corncake and ate the cake and washed the whole down with a drink of pulque.

Kino was finished and was rolling a cigarette when Juana spoke sharply. "Kino." He glanced at her and then got up and went quickly to her for he saw fright in her eyes. He stood over her, looking down, but the light was very dim. He kicked a pile of twigs into the fire hole to make a blaze, and then he could see the face of Coyotito. The baby's face was flushed and his throat was working and a little thick drool of saliva issued from his lips. The spasm of the stomach muscles began, and the baby was very sick.

Kino knelt beside his wife. "So the doctor knew," he said, but he said it for himself as well as for his wife, for his mind was hard and suspicious and he was remembering the white powder. Juana rocked from side to side and moaned out the little Song of the Family as though it could ward off the danger, and the baby vomited and writhed in her arms. Now uncertainty was in Kino, and the music of evil throbbed in his head and nearly drove out Juana's song.

The doctor finished his chocolate and nibbled the little fallen pieces of sweet cake. He brushed his fingers on a napkin, looked at his watch, arose, and took up his little bag.

The news of the baby's illness traveled quickly among the brush houses, for sickness is second only to hunger as the enemy of poor people. And some said softly, "Luck, you see, brings bitter friends." And they nodded and got up to go to Kino's house. The neighbors scuttled with covered noses through the dark until they crowded into Kino's house again. They stood and gazed, and they made little comments on the sadness that this should happen at a time of joy, and they said, "All things are in God's hands." The old women squatted down beside Juana to try to give her aid if they could and comfort if they could not.

Then the doctor hurried in, followed by his man. He scattered the old women like chickens. He took the baby and examined it and felt its head. "The poison it has worked," he said. "I think I can defeat it. I will try my best." He asked for water, and in the cup of it he put three drops of ammonia, and he pried open the baby's mouth and poured it down. The baby spluttered and screeched under the treatment, and Juana watched him with haunted eyes. The doctor spoke a little as he worked. "It is lucky that I know about the poison of the scorpion, otherwise—" and he shrugged to show what could have happened.

But Kino was suspicious, and he could not take his eyes from the doctor's open bag, and from the bottle of white powder there. Gradually the spasms subsided and the baby relaxed under the doctor's hands. And then Coyotito sighed deeply and went to sleep, for he was very tired with vomiting.

The doctor put the baby in Juana's arms. "He will get well now," he said. "I have won the fight." And Juana looked at him with adoration.

The doctor was closing his bag now. He said, "When do you think you can pay this bill?" He said it even kindly.

"When I have sold my pearl I will pay you," Kino said.

"You have a pearl? A good pearl?" the doctor asked with interest.

And then the chorus of the neighbors broke in.

"He has found the Pearl of the World," they cried, and they joined forefinger with thumb to show how great the pearl was.

"Kino will be a rich man," they clamored. "It is a pearl such as one has never seen."

The doctor looked surprised. "I had not heard of it. Do you keep this pearl in a safe place? Perhaps you would like me to put it in my safe?"

Kino's eyes were hooded now, his cheeks were drawn taut. "I have it secure," he said. "Tomorrow I will sell it and then I will pay you."

The doctor shrugged, and his wet eyes never left Kino's eyes. He knew the pearl would be buried in the house, and he thought Kino might look toward the place where it was buried. "It would be a shame to have it stolen before you could sell it," the doctor said, and he saw Kino's eyes flick involuntarily to the floor near the side post of the brush house.

When the doctor had gone and all the neighbors had reluctantly returned to their houses, Kino squatted beside the little glowing coals in the fire hole and listened to the night sound, the soft sweep of the little waves on the shore and the distant barking of dogs, the creeping of the breeze through the brush-house roof and the soft speech of his neighbors in their houses in the village. For these people do not sleep soundly all night; they awaken at intervals and talk a little and then go to sleep again. And after a while Kino got up and went to the door of his house.

He smelled the breeze and he listened for any foreign sound of secrecy or creeping, and his eyes searched the darkness, for the music of evil was sounding in his head and he was fierce and afraid. After he had probed the night with his senses he went to the place by the side post where the pearl was buried, and he dug it up and brought it to his sleeping mat, and under his sleeping mat he dug another little hole in the dirt floor and buried his pearl and covered it up again.

And Juana, sitting by the fire hole, watched him with questioning eyes, and when he had buried his pearl she asked, "Who do you fear?"

Kino searched for a true answer, and at last he said, "Everyone." And he could feel a shell of hardness drawing over him.

After a while they lay down together on the sleeping mat, and Juana did not put the baby in his box tonight, but cradled him on her arms and covered his face with her head shawl. And the last light went out of the embers in the fire hole.

But Kino's brain burned, even during his sleep, and he dreamed that Coyotito could read, that one of his own people could tell him the truth of things. And in his dream, Coyotito was reading from a book as large as a house, with letters as big as dogs, and the words galloped and played on the book. And then darkness spread over the page, and with the darkness came the music of evil again, and Kino stirred in his sleep; and when he stirred, Juana's eyes opened in the darkness. And then Kino awakened, with the evil music pulsing in him, and he lay in the darkness with his ears alert.

Then from the corner of the house came a sound so soft that it might have been simply a thought, a little furtive movement, a touch of a foot on earth, the almost inaudible purr of controlled breathing. Kino held his breath to listen, and he knew that whatever dark thing was in his house was holding its breath too, to listen. For a time no sound at all came from the corner of the brush house. Then Kino might have thought he had imagined the sound. But Juana's hand came creeping over to him in warning, and then the sound came again! The whisper of a foot on dry earth and the scratch of fingers in the soil.

And now a wild fear surged in Kino's breast, and on the fear came rage, as it always did. Kino's hand crept into his breast where his knife hung on a string, and then he sprang like an angry cat, leaped striking and spitting for the dark thing he knew was in the corner of the house. He felt cloth, struck at it with his knife and missed, and struck again and felt his knife go through cloth, and then his head crashed with lightning and exploded with pain. There was a soft scurry in the doorway, and running steps for a moment, and then silence.

Kino could feel warm blood running down from his forehead, and he could hear Juana calling to him. "Kino! Kino!" And there was terror in her voice. Then coldness came over him as quickly as the rage had, and he said, "I am all right. The thing has gone."

He groped his way back to the sleeping mat. Already Juana was working at the fire. She uncovered an ember from the ashes and shredded little pieces of cornhusk over it and blew a little flame into the cornhusks so that a tiny light danced through the hut. And then from a secret place Juana brought a little piece of consecrated candle and lighted it at the flame and set it upright on a fireplace stone. She worked quickly, crooning as she moved about. She dipped the end of her head shawl in water and swabbed the blood from Kino's bruised forehead. "It is nothing," Kino said, but his eyes and his voice were hard and cold and a brooding hate was growing in him.

Now the tension which had been growing in Juana boiled up to the surface and her lips were thin. "This thing is evil," she cried harshly. "This pearl is like a sin! It will destroy us," and her voice rose shrilly. "Throw it away, Kino. Let us break it between stones. Let us bury it and forget the place. Let us throw it back into the sea. It has brought evil. Kino, my husband, it will destroy us." And in the firelight her lips and her eyes were alive with her fear.

But Kino's face was set, and his mind and his will were set. "This is our one chance," he said. "Our son must go to school. He must break out of the pot that holds us in."

"It will destroy us all," Juana cried. "Even our son."

"Hush," said Kino. "Do not speak any more. In the morning we will sell the pearl, and then the evil will be gone, and only the good remain. Now hush, my wife." His dark eyes scowled into the little fire, and for the first time he knew that his knife was still in his hands, and he raised the blade and looked at it and saw a little line of blood on the steel. For a moment he seemed about to wipe the blade on his trousers but then he plunged the knife into the earth and so cleansed it.

The distant roosters began to crow and the air changed and the dawn was coming. The wind of the morning ruffled the water of the estuary and whispered through the mangroves, and the little waves beat on the rubbly beach with an increased tempo. Kino raised the sleeping mat and dug up his pearl and put it in front of him and stared at it.

And the beauty of the pearl, winking and glimmering in the light of the little candle, cozened his brain with its beauty. So lovely it was, so soft, and its own music came from it—its music of promise and delight, its guarantee of the future, of comfort, of security. Its warm lucence promised a poultice against illness and a wall against insult. It closed a door on hunger. And as he stared at it Kino's eyes softened and his face relaxed. He could see the little image of the consecrated candle reflected in the soft surface of the pearl, and he heard again in his ears the lovely music of the undersea, the tone of the diffused green light of the sea bottom. Juana, glancing secretly at him, saw him smile. And because they were in some way one thing and one purpose, she smiled with him.

And they began this day with hope.

I T IS wonderful the way a little town keeps track of itself and of all its units. If every single man and woman,
child and baby, acts and conducts itself in a known pattern and breaks no walls and differs with no one and experi-
ments in no way and is not sick and does not endanger the
ease and peace of mind or steady unbroken flow of the
town, then that unit can disappear and never be heard of.
But let one man step out of the regular thought or the
known and trusted pattern, and the nerves of the towns-
people ring with nervousness and communication travels
over the nerve lines of the town. Then every unit communi-
cates to the whole.

Thus, in La Paz, it was known in the early morning
through the whole town that Kino was going to sell his
pearl that day. It was known among the neighbors in the
brush huts, among the pearl fishermen; it was known among
the Chinese grocery-store owners; it was known in the
church, for the altar boys whispered about it. Word of it
crept in among the nuns; the beggars in front of the church
spoke of it, for they would be there to take the tithe of the
first fruits of the luck. The little boys knew about it with
excitement, but most of all the pearl buyers knew about it,
and when the day had come, in the offices of the pearl buyers, each man sat alone with his little black velvet tray, and
each man rolled the pearls about with his fingertips and
considered his part in the picture.

It was supposed that the pearl buyers were individuals
acting alone, bidding against one another for the pearls the
fishermen brought in. And once it had been so. But this was
a wasteful method, for often, in the excitement of bidding
for a fine pearl, too great a price had been paid to the fisher-

men. This was extravagant and not to be countenanced. Now there was only one pearl buyer with many hands, and the men who sat in their offices and waited for Kino knew what price they would offer, how high they would bid, and what method each one would use. And although these men would not profit beyond their salaries, there was excitement among the pearl buyers, for there was excitement in the hunt, and if it be a man's function to break down a price, then he must take joy and satisfaction in breaking it as far down as possible. For every man in the world functions to the best of his ability, and no one does less than his best, no matter what he may think about it. Quite apart from any reward they might get, from any word of praise, from any promotion, a pearl buyer was a pearl buyer, and the best and happiest pearl buyer was he who bought for the lowest prices.

The sun was hot yellow that morning, and it drew the moisture from the estuary and from the Gulf and hung it in shimmering scarves in the air so that the air vibrated and vision was insubstantial. A vision hung in the air to the north of the city—the vision of a mountain that was over two hundred miles away, and the high slopes of this mountain were swaddled with pines and a great stone peak arose above the timber line.

And the morning of this day the canoes lay lined up on the beach; the fishermen did not go out to dive for pearls, for there would be too much happening, too many things to see when Kino went to sell the great pearl.

In the brush houses by the shore Kino's neighbors sat long over their breakfasts, and they spoke of what they would do if they had found the pearl. And one man said that he would give it as a present to the Holy Father in Rome. Another said that he would buy Masses for the souls of his family for a thousand years. Another thought he might take the money and distribute it among the poor of

La Paz; and a fourth thought of all the good things one could do with the money from the pearl, of all the charities, benefits, of all the rescues one could perform if one had money. All of the neighbors hoped that sudden wealth would not turn Kino's head, would not make a rich man of him, would not graft onto him the evil limbs of greed and hatred and coldness. For Kino was a well-liked man; it would be a shame if the pearl destroyed him. "That good wife Juana," they said, "and the beautiful baby Coyotito, and the others to come. What a pity it would be if the pearl should destroy them all."

For Kino and Juana this was the morning of mornings of their lives, comparable only to the day when the baby had been born. This was to be the day from which all other days would take their arrangement. Thus they would say, "It was two years before we sold the pearl," or, "It was six weeks after we sold the pearl." Juana, considering the matter, threw caution to the winds, and she dressed Coyotito in the clothes she had prepared for his baptism, when there would be money for his baptism. And Juana combed and braided her hair and tied the ends with two little bows of red ribbon, and she put on her marriage skirt and waist. The sun was quarter high when they were ready. Kino's ragged white clothes were clean at least, and this was the last day of his raggedness. For tomorrow, or even this afternoon, he would have new clothes.

The neighbors, watching Kino's door through the crevices in their brush houses, were dressed and ready too. There was no self-consciousness about their joining Kino and Juana to go pearl selling. It was expected, it was a historic moment, they would be crazy if they didn't go. It would be almost a sign of unfriendship.

Juana put on her head shawl carefully, and she draped one long end under her right elbow and gathered it with her right hand so that a hammock hung under her arm, and in this little hammock she placed Coyotito, propped up against the head shawl so that he could see everything and perhaps remember. Kino put on his large straw hat and felt it with his hand to see that it was properly placed, not on the back or side of his head, like a rash, unmarried, irresponsible man, and not flat as an elder would wear it, but tilted a little forward to show aggressiveness and seriousness and vigor. There is a great deal to be seen in the tilt of a hat on a man. Kino slipped his feet into his sandals and pulled the thongs up over his heels. The great pearl was wrapped in an old soft piece of deerskin and placed in a little leather bag, and the leather bag was in a pocket in Kino's shirt. He folded his blanket carefully and draped it in a narrow strip over his left shoulder, and now they were ready.

Kino stepped with dignity out of the house, and Juana followed him, carrying Coyotito. And as they marched up the freshet-washed alley toward the town, the neighbors joined them. The houses belched people; the doorways spewed out children. But because of the seriousness of the occasion, only one man walked with Kino, and that was his brother, Juan Tomás.

Juan Tomás cautioned his brother. "You must be careful to see they do not cheat you," he said.

And, "Very careful," Kino agreed.

"We do not know what prices are paid in other places," said Juan Tomás. "How can we know what is a fair price, if we do not know what the pearl buyer gets for the pearl in another place."

"That is true," said Kino, "but how can we know? We are here, we are not there."

As they walked up toward the city the crowd grew behind them, and Juan Tomás, in pure nervousness, went on speaking.

"Before you were born, Kino," he said, "the old ones thought of a way to get more money for their pearls. They thought it would be better if they had an agent who took all the pearls to the capital and sold them there and kept only his share of the profit."

Kino nodded his head. "I know," he said. "It was a good thought."

"And so they got such a man," said Juan Tomás, "and they pooled the pearls, and they started him off. And he was never heard of again and the pearls were lost. Then they got another man, and they started him off, and he was never heard of again. And so they gave the whole thing up and went back to the old way."

"I know," said Kino. "I have heard our father tell of it. It was a good idea, but it was against religion, and the Father made that very clear. The loss of the pearl was a punishment visited on those who tried to leave their station. And the Father made it clear that each man and woman is like a soldier sent by God to guard some part of the castle of the Universe. And some are in the ramparts and some far deep in the darkness of the walls. But each one must remain faithful to his post and must not go running about, else the castle is in danger from the assaults of Hell."

"I have heard him make that sermon," said Juan Tomás. "He makes it every year."

The brothers, as they walked along, squinted their eyes a little, as they and their grandfathers and their great-grandfathers had done for four hundred years, since first the strangers came with argument and authority and gunpowder to back up both. And in the four hundred years Kino's people had learned only one defense—a slight slitting of the eyes and a slight tightening of the lips and a retirement. Nothing could break down this wall, and they could remain whole within the wall.

The gathering procession was solemn, for they sensed the importance of this day, and any children who showed a tendency to scuffle, to scream, to cry out, to steal hats and rumple hair, were hissed to silence by their elders. So important was this day that an old man came to see, riding on the stalwart shoulders of his nephew. The procession left the brush huts and entered the stone and plaster city where the streets were a little wider and there were narrow pavements beside the buildings. And as before, the beggars joined them as they passed the church; the grocers looked out at them as they went by; the little saloons lost their customers and the owners closed up shop and went along. And the sun beat down on the streets of the city and even tiny stones threw shadows on the ground.

The news of the approach of the procession ran ahead of it, and in their little dark offices the pearl buyers stiffened and grew alert. They got out papers so that they could be at work when Kino appeared, and they put their pearls in the desks, for it is not good to let an inferior pearl be seen beside a beauty. And word of the loveliness of Kino's pearl had come to them. The pearl buyers' offices were clustered together in one narrow street, and they were barred at the windows, and wooden slats cut out the light so that only a soft gloom entered the offices.

A stout slow man sat in an office waiting. His face was fatherly and benign, and his eyes twinkled with friendship. He was a caller of good mornings, a ceremonious shaker of hands, a jolly man who knew all jokes and yet who hovered close to sadness, for in the midst of a laugh he could remember the death of your aunt, and his eyes could become wet with sorrow for your loss. This morning he had placed a flower in a vase on his desk, a single scarlet hibiscus, and the vase sat beside the black velvet-lined pearl tray in front of him. He was shaved close to the blue roots of his beard, and his hands were clean and his nails polished. His door stood open to the morning, and he hummed under his breath while his right hand practiced legerdemain. He rolled a coin back and forth over his knuckles and made it appear and disappear, made it spin and sparkle. The coin winked into sight and as quickly slipped out of sight, and the man did not even watch his own performance. The fingers did it all mechanically, precisely, while the man hummed to himself and peered out the door. Then he heard the tramp of feet of the approaching crowd, and the fingers of his right hand worked faster and faster until, as the figure of Kino filled the doorway, the coin flashed and disappeared.

"Good morning, my friend," the stout man said. "What can I do for you?"

Kino stared into the dimness of the little office, for his eyes were squeezed from the outside glare. But the buyer's eyes had become as steady and cruel and unwinking as a hawk's eyes, while the rest of his face smiled in greeting. And secretly, behind his desk, his right hand practiced with the coin.

"I have a pearl," said Kino. And Juan Tomás stood beside him and snorted a little at the understatement. The neighbors peered around the doorway, and a line of little boys clambered on the window bars and looked through. Several little boys, on their hands and knees, watched the scene around Kino's legs.

"You have a pearl," the dealer said. "Sometimes a man brings in a dozen. Well, let us see your pearl. We will value it and give you the best price." And his fingers worked furiously with the coin.

Now Kino instinctively knew his own dramatic effects. Slowly he brought out the leather bag, slowly took from it the soft and dirty piece of deerskin, and then he let the great pearl roll into the black velvet tray, and instantly his eyes went to the buyer's face. But there was no sign, no movement, the face did not change, but the secret hand behind the desk missed in its precision. The coin stumbled over a knuckle and slipped silently into the dealer's lap. And the fingers behind the desk curled into a fist. When the right hand came out of hiding, the forefinger touched the great pearl, rolled it on the black velvet; thumb and forefinger picked it up and brought it near to the dealer's eyes and twirled it in the air.

Kino held his breath, and the neighbors held their breath, and the whispering went back through the crowd. "He is inspecting it— No price has been mentioned yet— They have not come to a price."

Now the dealer's hand had become a personality. The hand tossed the great pearl back in the tray, the forefinger poked and insulted it, and on the dealer's face there came a sad and contemptuous smile.

"I am sorry, my friend," he said, and his shoulders rose a little to indicate that the misfortune was no fault of his.

"It is a pearl of great value," Kino said.

The dealer's fingers spurned the pearl so that it bounced and rebounded softly from the side of the velvet tray.

"You have heard of fool's gold," the dealer said. "This pearl is like fool's gold. It is too large. Who would buy it? There is no market for such things. It is a curiosity only. I am sorry. You thought it was a thing of value, and it is only a curiosity."

Now Kino's face was perplexed and worried. "It is the Pearl of the World," he cried. "No one has ever seen such a pearl."

"On the contrary," said the dealer, "it is large and clumsy. As a curiosity it has interest; some museum might perhaps take it to place in a collection of seashells. I can give you, say, a thousand pesos."

Kino's face grew dark and dangerous. "It is worth fifty thousand," he said. "You know it. You want to cheat me."

And the dealer heard a little grumble go through the crowd as they heard his price. And the dealer felt a little tremor of fear.

"Do not blame me," he said quickly. "I am only an appraiser. Ask the others. Go to their offices and show your pearl—or better let them come here, so that you can see there is no collusion. Boy," he called. And when his servant looked through the rear door, "Boy, go to such a one, and such another one and such a third one. Ask them to step in here and do not tell them why. Just say that I will be pleased to see them." And his right hand went behind the desk and pulled another coin from his pocket, and the coin rolled back and forth over the knuckles.

Kino's neighbors whispered together. They had been afraid of something like this. The pearl was large, but it had a strange color. They had been suspicious of it from the first. And after all, a thousand pesos was not to be thrown away. It was comparative wealth to a man who was not wealthy. And suppose Kino took a thousand pesos. Only yesterday he had nothing.

But Kino had grown tight and hard. He felt the creeping of fate, the circling of wolves, the hover of vultures. He felt the evil coagulating about him, and he was helpless to protect himself. He heard in his ears the evil music. And on the black velvet the great pearl glistened, so that the dealer could not keep his eyes from it.

The crowd in the doorway wavered and broke and let the three pearl dealers through. The crowd was silent now, fearing to miss a word, to fail to see a gesture or an expression. Kino was silent and watchful. He felt a little tugging at his back, and he turned and looked in Juana's eyes, and when he looked away he had renewed strength.

The dealers did not glance at one another nor at the pearl. The man behind the desk said, "I have put a value on this pearl. The owner here does not think it fair. I will ask you to examine this—this thing and make an offer. Notice," he said to Kino, "I have not mentioned what I have offered."

The first dealer, dry and stringy, seemed now to see the pearl for the first time. He took it up, rolled it quickly be-

tween thumb and forefinger, and then cast it contemptuously back into the tray.

"Do not include me in the discussion," he said dryly. "I
will make no offer at all. I do not want it. This is not a pearl
—it is a monstrosity." His thin lips curled.

Now the second dealer, a little man with a shy soft voice,
took up the pearl, and he examined it carefully. He took a
glass from his pocket and inspected it under magnification.
Then he laughed softly.

"Better pearls are made of paste," he said. "I know these
things. This is soft and chalky, it will lose its color and die
in a few months. Look." He offered the glass to Kino,
showed him how to use it, and Kino, who had never seen a
pearl's surface magnified, was shocked at the strange-looking
surface.

The third dealer took the pearl from Kino's hands. "One
of my clients likes such things," he said. "I will offer five
hundred pesos, and perhaps I can sell it to my client for six
hundred."

Kino reached quickly and snatched the pearl from his
hand. He wrapped it in the deerskin and thrust it inside his
shirt.

The man behind the desk said, "I'm a fool, I know, but
my first offer stands. I still offer one thousand. What are
you doing?" he asked, as Kino thrust the pearl out of sight.

"I am cheated," Kino cried fiercely. "My pearl is not for
sale here. I will go, perhaps even to the capital."

Now the dealers glanced quickly at one another. They
knew they had played too hard; they knew they would be
disciplined for their failure, and the man at the desk said
quickly, "I might go to fifteen hundred."

But Kino was pushing his way through the crowd. The
hum of talk came to him dimly, his rage blood pounded in
his ears, and he burst through and strode away. Juana followed, trotting after him.

When the evening came, the neighbors in the brush houses sat eating their corncakes and beans, and they discussed the great theme of the morning. They did not know, it seemed a fine pearl to them, but they had never seen such a pearl before, and surely the dealers knew more about the value of pearls than they. "And mark this," they said. "Those dealers did not discuss these things. Each of the three knew the pearl was valueless."

"But suppose they had arranged it before?"

"If that is so, then all of us have been cheated all of our lives."

Perhaps, some argued, perhaps it would have been better if Kino took the one thousand five hundred pesos. That is a great deal of money, more than he has ever seen. Maybe Kino is being a pigheaded fool. Suppose he should really go to the capital and find no buyer for his pearl. He would never live that down.

And now, said other fearful ones, now that he had defied them, those buyers will not want to deal with him at all. Maybe Kino has cut off his own head and destroyed himself.

And others said, Kino is a brave man, and a fierce man; he is right. From his courage we may all profit. These were proud of Kino.

In his house Kino squatted on his sleeping mat, brooding. He had buried his pearl under a stone of the fire hole in his house, and he stared at the woven tules of his sleeping mat until the crossed design danced in his head. He had lost one world and had not gained another. And Kino was afraid. Never in his life had he been far from home. He was afraid of strangers and of strange places. He was terrified of that monster of strangeness they called the capital. It lay over the water and through the mountains, over a thousand miles, and every strange terrible mile was frightening. But Kino had lost his old world and he must clamber on to a new one.

For his dream of the future was real and never to be destroyed, and he had said "I will go," and that made a real thing too. To determine to go and to say it was to be halfway there.

Juana watched him while he buried his pearl, and she watched him while she cleaned Coyotito and nursed him, and Juana made the corncakes for supper.

Juan Tomás came in and squatted down beside Kino and remained silent for a long time, until at last Kino demanded, "What else could I do? They are cheats."

Juan Tomás nodded gravely. He was the elder, and Kino looked to him for wisdom. "It is hard to know," he said. "We do know that we are cheated from birth to the overcharge on our coffins. But we survive. You have defied not the pearl buyers, but the whole structure, the whole way of life, and I am afraid for you."

"What have I to fear but starvation?" Kino asked.

But Juan Tomás shook his head slowly. "That we must all fear. But suppose you are correct—suppose your pearl is of great value—do you think then the game is over?"

"What do you mean?"

"I don't know," said Juan Tomás, "but I am afraid for you. It is new ground you are walking on, you do not know the way."

"I will go. I will go soon," said Kino.

"Yes," Juan Tomás agreed. "That you must do. But I wonder if you will find it any different in the capital. Here, you have friends and me, your brother. There, you will have no one."

"What can I do?" Kino cried. "Some deep outrage is here. My son must have a chance. That is what they are striking at. My friends will protect me."

"Only so long as they are not in danger or discomfort from it," said Juan Tomás. He arose, saying, "Go with God."

And Kino said, "Go with God," and did not even look up, for the words had a strange chill in them.

Long after Juan Tomás had gone Kino sat brooding on his sleeping mat. A lethargy had settled on him, and a little gray hopelessness. Every road seemed blocked against him. In his head he heard only the dark music of the enemy. His senses were burningly alive, but his mind went back to the deep participation with all things, the gift he had from his people. He heard every little sound of the gathering night, the sleepy complaint of settling birds, the love agony of cats, the strike and withdrawal of little waves on the beach, and the simple hiss of distance. And he could smell the sharp odor of exposed kelp from the receding tide. The little flare of the twig fire made the design on his sleeping mat jump before his entranced eyes.

Juana watched him with worry, but she knew him and she knew she could help him best by being silent and by being near. And as though she too could hear the Song of Evil, she fought it, singing softly the melody of the family, of the safety and warmth and wholeness of the family. She held Coyotito in her arms and sang the song to him, to keep the evil out, and her voice was brave against the threat of the dark music.

Kino did not move nor ask for his supper. She knew he would ask when he wanted it. His eyes were entranced, and he could sense the wary, watchful evil outside the brush house; he could feel the dark creeping things waiting for him to go out into the night. It was shadowy and dreadful, and yet it called to him and threatened him and challenged him. His right hand went into his shirt and felt his knife; his eyes were wide; he stood up and walked to the doorway.

Juana willed to stop him; she raised her hand to stop him, and her mouth opened with terror. For a long moment Kino looked out into the darkness and then he stepped outside. Juana heard the little rush, the grunting struggle, the blow.

She froze with terror for a moment, and then her lips drew back from her teeth like a cat's lips. She set Coyotito down on the ground. She seized a stone from the fireplace and rushed outside, but it was over by then. Kino lay on the ground, struggling to rise, and there was no one near him. Only the shadows and the strike and rush of waves and the hiss of distance. But the evil was all about, hidden behind the brush fence, crouched beside the house in the shadow, hovering in the air.

Juana dropped her stone, and she put her arms around Kino and helped him to his feet and supported him into the house. Blood oozed down from his scalp and there was a long deep cut in his cheek from ear to chin, a deep, bleeding slash. And Kino was only half conscious. He shook his head from side to side. His shirt was torn open and his clothes half pulled off. Juana sat him down on his sleeping mat and she wiped the thickening blood from his face with her skirt. She brought him pulque to drink in a little pitcher, and still he shook his head to clear out the darkness.

"Who?" Juana asked.

"I don't know," Kino said. "I didn't see."

Now Juana brought her clay pot of water and she washed the cut on his face while he stared dazed ahead of him.

"Kino, my husband," she cried, and his eyes stared past her. "Kino, can you hear me?"

"I hear you," he said dully.

"Kino, this pearl is evil. Let us destroy it before it destroys us. Let us crush it between two stones. Let us—let us throw it back in the sea where it belongs. Kino, it is evil, it is evil!"

And as she spoke the light came back in Kino's eyes so that they glowed fiercely and his muscles hardened and his will hardened.

"No," he said. "I will fight this thing. I will win over it. We will have our chance." His fist pounded the sleeping mat. "No one shall take our good fortune from us," he said. His eyes softened then and he raised a gentle hand to Juana's shoulder. "Believe me," he said. "I am a man." And his face grew crafty.

"In the morning we will take our canoe and we will go over the sea and over the mountains to the capital, you and I. We will not be cheated. I am a man."

"Kino," she said huskily, "I am afraid. A man can be killed. Let us throw the pearl back into the sea."

"Hush," he said fiercely. "I am a man. Hush." And she was silent, for his voice was command. "Let us sleep a little," he said. "In the first light we will start. You are not afraid to go with me?"

"No, my husband."

His eyes were soft and warm on her then, his hand touched her cheek. "Let us sleep a little," he said.

THE late moon arose before the first rooster crowed. Kino opened his eyes in the darkness, for he sensed movement near him, but he did not move. Only his eyes searched the darkness, and in the pale light of the moon that crept through the holes in the brush house Kino saw Juana arise silently from beside him. He saw her move toward the fireplace. So carefully did she work that he heard only the lightest sound when she moved the fireplace stone. And then like a shadow she glided toward the door. She paused for a moment beside the hanging box where Coyotito lay, then for a second she was black in the doorway, and then she was gone.

And rage surged in Kino. He rolled up to his feet and followed her as silently as she had gone, and he could hear her quick footsteps going toward the shore. Quietly he tracked her, and his brain was red with anger. She burst clear out of the brush line and stumbled over the little boulders toward the water, and then she heard him coming and she broke into a run. Her arm was up to throw when he leaped at her and caught her arm and wrenched the pearl from her. He struck her in the face with his clenched fist and she fell among the boulders, and he kicked her in the side. In the pale light he could see the little waves break over her, and her skirt floated about and clung to her legs as the water receded.

Kino looked down at her and his teeth were bared. He hissed at her like a snake, and Juana stared at him with wide unfrightened eyes, like a sheep before the butcher. She knew there was murder in him, and it was all right; she had accepted it, and she would not resist or even protest. And then the rage left him and a sick disgust took its place. He turned away from her and walked up the beach and through the brush line. His senses were dulled by his emotion.

He heard the rush, got his knife out and lunged at one dark figure and felt his knife go home, and then he was swept to his knees and swept again to the ground. Greedy fingers went through his clothes, frantic fingers searched him, and the pearl, knocked from his hand, lay winking behind a little stone in the pathway. It glinted in the soft moonlight.

Juana dragged herself up from the rocks on the edge of the water. Her face was a dull pain and her side ached. She steadied herself on her knees for a while and her wet skirt clung to her. There was no anger in her for Kino. He had said, "I am a man," and that meant certain things to Juana. It meant that he was half insane and half god. It meant that Kino would drive his strength against a mountain and plunge his strength against the sea. Juana, in her woman's soul, knew that the mountain would stand while the man broke himself; that the sea would surge while the man drowned in it. And yet it was this thing that made him a man, half insane and half god, and Juana had need of a man; she could not live without a man. Although she might be puzzled by these differences between man and woman, she knew them and accepted them and needed them. Of course she would follow him, there was no question of that. Sometimes the quality of woman, the reason, the caution, the sense of preservation, could cut through Kino's manness and save them all. She climbed painfully to her feet, and she dipped her cupped palms in the little waves and washed her bruised face with the stinging salt water, and then she went creeping up the beach after Kino.

A flight of herring clouds had moved over the sky from the south. The pale moon dipped in and out of the strands of clouds so that Juana walked in darkness for a moment and light the next. Her back was bent with pain and her head was low. She went through the line of brush when the moon was covered, and when it looked through she saw the glimmer of the great pearl in the path behind the rock. She sank to her knees and picked it up, and the moon went into the darkness of the clouds again. Juana remained on her knees while she considered whether to go back to the sea and finish her job, and as she considered, the light came again, and she saw two dark figures lying in the path ahead of her. She leaped forward and saw that one was Kino and the other a stranger with dark shiny fluid leaking from his throat.

Kino moved sluggishly, arms and legs stirred like those of a crushed bug, and a thick muttering came from his mouth. Now, in an instant, Juana knew that the old life was gone forever. A dead man in the path and Kino's knife, dark bladed beside him, convinced her. All of the time Juana had been trying to rescue something of the old peace, of the time before the pearl. But now it was gone, and there was no retrieving it. And knowing this, she abandoned the past instantly. There was nothing to do but to save themselves.

Her pain was gone now, her slowness. Quickly she dragged the dead man from the pathway into the shelter of the brush. She went to Kino and sponged his face with her wet skirt. His senses were coming back and he moaned.

"They have taken the pearl. I have lost it. Now it is over," he said. "The pearl is gone."

Juana quieted him as she would quiet a sick child. "Hush," she said. "Here is your pearl. I found it in the path. Can you hear me now? Here is your pearl. Can you understand? You have killed a man. We must go away. They will come for us, can you understand? We must be gone before the daylight comes."

"I was attacked," Kino said uneasily. "I struck to save my life."

"Do you remember yesterday?" Juana asked. "Do you

think that will matter? Do you remember the men of the city? Do you think your explanation will help?"

Kino drew a great breath and fought off his weakness. "No," he said. "You are right." And his will hardened and he was a man again.

"Go to our house and bring Coyotito," he said, "and bring all the corn we have. I will drag the canoe into the water and we will go."

He took his knife and left her. He stumbled toward the beach and he came to his canoe. And when the light broke through again he saw that a great hole had been knocked in the bottom. And a searing rage came to him and gave him strength. Now the darkness was closing in on his family; now the evil music filled the night, hung over the mangroves, skirled in the wave beat. The canoe of his grandfather, plastered over and over, and a splintered hole broken in it. This was an evil beyond thinking. The killing of a man was not so evil as the killing of a boat. For a boat does not have sons, and a boat cannot protect itself, and a wounded boat does not heal. There was sorrow in Kino's rage, but this last thing had tightened him beyond breaking. He was an animal now, for hiding, for attacking, and he lived only to preserve himself and his family. He was not conscious of the pain in his head. He leaped up the beach, through the brush line toward his brush house, and it did not occur to him to take one of the canoes of his neighbors. Never once did the thought enter his head, any more than he could have conceived breaking a boat.

The roosters were crowing and the dawn was not far off. Smoke of the first fires seeped out through the walls of the brush houses, and the first smell of cooking corncakes was in the air. Already the dawn birds were scampering in the bushes. The weak moon was losing its light and the clouds thickened and curdled to the southward. The wind blew freshly into the estuary, a nervous, restless wind with the

smell of storm on its breath, and there was change and un-
easiness in the air.

Kino, hurrying toward his house, felt a surge of exhilaration. Now he was not confused, for there was only one
thing to do, and Kino's hand went first to the great pearl in
his shirt and then to his knife hanging under his shirt.

He saw a little glow ahead of him, and then without interval a tall flame leaped up in the dark with a crackling
roar, and a tall edifice of fire lighted the pathway. Kino
broke into a run; it was his brush house, he knew. And he
knew that these houses could burn down in a very few moments. And as he ran a scuttling figure ran toward him—
Juana, with Coyotito in her arms and Kino's shoulder
blanket clutched in her hand. The baby moaned with fright,
and Juana's eyes were wide and terrified. Kino could see the
house was gone, and he did not question Juana. He knew,
but she said, "It was torn up and the floor dug—even the
baby's box turned out, and as I looked they put the fire to
the outside."

The fierce light of the burning house lighted Kino's face
strongly. "Who?" he demanded.

"I don't know," she said. "The dark ones."

The neighbors were tumbling from their houses now, and
they watched the falling sparks and stamped them out to
save their own houses. Suddenly Kino was afraid. The light
made him afraid. He remembered the man lying dead in the
brush beside the path, and he took Juana by the arm and
drew her into the shadow of a house away from the light,
for light was danger to him. For a moment he considered
and then he worked among the shadows until he came to
the house of Juan Tomás, his brother, and he slipped into
the doorway and drew Juana after him. Outside, he could
hear the squeal of children and the shouts of the neighbors,
for his friends thought he might be inside the burning house.

The house of Juan Tomás was almost exactly like Kino's

house; nearly all the brush houses were alike, and all leaked light and air, so that Juana and Kino, sitting in the corner of the brother's house, could see the leaping flames through the wall. They saw the flames tall and furious, they saw the roof fall and watched the fire die down as quickly as a twig fire dies. They heard the cries of warning of their friends, and the shrill, keening cry of Apolonia, wife of Juan Tomás. She, being the nearest woman relative, raised a formal lament for the dead of the family.

Apolonia realized that she was wearing her second-best head shawl and she rushed to her house to get her fine new one. As she rummaged in a box by the wall, Kino's voice said quietly, "Apolonia, do not cry out. We are not hurt."

"How do you come here?" she demanded.

"Do not question," he said. "Go now to Juan Tomás and bring him here and tell no one else. This is important to us, Apolonia."

She paused, her hands helpless in front of her, and then, "Yes, my brother-in-law," she said.

In a few moments Juan Tomás came back with her. He lighted a candle and came to them where they crouched in a corner and he said, "Apolonia, see to the door, and do not let anyone enter." He was older, Juan Tomás, and he assumed the authority. "Now, my brother," he said.

"I was attacked in the dark," said Kino. "And in the fight I have killed a man."

"Who?" asked Juan Tomás quickly.

"I do not know. It is all darkness—all darkness and the shape of darkness."

"It is the pearl," said Juan Tomás. "There is a devil in this pearl. You should have sold it and passed on the devil. Perhaps you can still sell it and buy peace for yourself."

And Kino said, "Oh, my brother, an insult has been put on me that is deeper than my life. For on the beach my canoe is broken, my house is burned, and in the brush a dead man lies. Every escape is cut off. You must hide us, my brother."

And Kino, looking closely, saw deep worry come into his brother's eyes and he forestalled him in a possible refusal. "Not for long," he said quickly. "Only until a day has passed and the new night has come. Then we will go."

"I will hide you," said Juan Tomás.

"I do not want to bring danger to you," Kino said. "I know I am like a leprosy. I will go tonight and then you will be safe."

"I will protect you," said Juan Tomás, and he called, "Apolonia, close up the door. Do not even whisper that Kino is here."

They sat silently all day in the darkness of the house, and they could hear the neighbors speaking of them. Through the walls of the house they could watch their neighbors raking through the ashes to find the bones. Crouching in the house of Juan Tomás, they heard the shock go into their neighbors' minds at the news of the broken boat. Juan Tomás went out among the neighbors to divert their suspicions, and he gave them theories and ideas of what had happened to Kino and to Juana and to the baby. To one he said, "I think they have gone south along the coast to escape the evil that was on them." And to another, "Kino would never leave the sea. Perhaps he found another boat." And he said, "Apolonia is ill with grief."

And on that day the wind rose up to beat the Gulf and tore the kelps and weeds that lined the shore, and the wind cried through the brush houses and no boat was safe on the water. Then Juan Tomás told among the neighbors, "Kino is gone. If he went to the sea, he is drowned by now." And after each trip among the neighbors Juan Tomás came back with something borrowed. He brought a little woven straw bag of red beans and a gourd full of rice. He borrowed a cup of dried peppers and a block of salt, and he brought in a long working knife, eighteen inches long and heavy, as a small ax, a tool and a weapon. And when Kino saw this knife his eyes lighted up, and he fondled the blade and his thumb tested the edge.

The wind screamed over the Gulf and turned the water white, and the mangroves plunged like frightened cattle, and a fine sandy dust arose from the land and hung in a stifling cloud over the sea. The wind drove off the clouds and skimmed the sky clean and drifted the sand of the country like snow.

Then Juan Tomás, when the evening approached, talked long with his brother. "Where will you go?"

"To the north," said Kino. "I have heard that there are cities in the north."

"Avoid the shore," said Juan Tomás. "They are making a party to search the shore. The men in the city will look for you. Do you still have the pearl?"

"I have it," said Kino. "And I will keep it. I might have given it as a gift, but now it is my misfortune and my life and I will keep it." His eyes were hard and cruel and bitter.

Coyotito whimpered and Juana muttered little magics over him to make him silent.

"The wind is good," said Juan Tomás. "There will be no tracks."

They left quietly in the dark before the moon had risen. The family stood formally in the house of Juan Tomás. Juana carried Coyotito on her back, covered and held in by her head shawl, and the baby slept, cheek turned sideways against her shoulder. The head shawl covered the baby, and one end of it came across Juana's nose to protect her from the evil night air. Juan Tomás embraced his brother with the double embrace and kissed him on both cheeks. "Go with God," he said, and it was like a death. "You will not give up the pearl?"

"This pearl has become my soul," said Kino. "If I give it up I shall lose my soul. Go thou also with God."

6.

THE wind blew fierce and strong, and it pelted them with bits of sticks, sand, and little rocks. Juana and Kino gathered their clothing tighter about them and covered their noses and went out into the world. The sky was brushed clean by the wind and the stars were cold in a black sky. The two walked carefully, and they avoided the center of the town where some sleeper in a doorway might see them pass. For the town closed itself in against the night, and anyone who moved about in the darkness would be noticeable. Kino threaded his way around the edge of the city and turned north, north by the stars, and found the rutted sandy road that led through the brushy country toward Loreto where the miraculous Virgin has her station.

Kino could feel the blown sand against his ankles and he was glad, for he knew there would be no tracks. The little light from the stars made out for him the narrow road through the brushy country. And Kino could hear the pad of Juana's feet behind him. He went quickly and quietly, and Juana trotted behind him to keep up.

Some ancient thing stirred in Kino. Through his fear of dark and the devils that haunt the night, there came a rush of exhilaration; some animal thing was moving in him so that he was cautious and wary and dangerous; some ancient thing out of the past of his people was alive in him. The wind was at his back and the stars guided him. The wind cried and whisked in the brush, and the family went on monotonously, hour after hour. They passed no one and saw no one. At last, to their right, the waning moon arose, and when it came up the wind died down, and the land was still.

Now they could see the little road ahead of them, deep

cut with sand-drifted wheel tracks. With the wind gone there would be footprints, but they were a good distance from the town and perhaps their tracks might not be noticed. Kino walked carefully in a wheel rut, and Juana followed in his path. One big cart, going to the town in the morning, could wipe out every trace of their passage.

All night they walked and never changed their pace. Once Coyotito awakened, and Juana shifted him in front of her and soothed him until he went to sleep again. And the evils of the night were about them. The coyotes cried and laughed in the brush, and the owls screeched and hissed over their heads. And once some large animal lumbered away, crackling the undergrowth as it went. And Kino gripped the handle of the big working knife and took a sense of protection from it.

The music of the pearl was triumphant in Kino's head, and the quiet melody of the family underlay it, and they wove themselves into the soft padding of sandaled feet in the dust. All night they walked, and in the first dawn Kino searched the roadside for a covert to lie in during the day. He found his place near to the road, a little clearing where deer might have lain, and it was curtained thickly with the dry brittle trees that lined the road. And when Juana had seated herself and had settled to nurse the baby, Kino went back to the road. He broke a branch and carefully swept the footprints where they had turned from the roadway. And then, in the first light, he heard the creak of a wagon, and he crouched beside the road and watched a heavy two-wheeled cart go by, drawn by slouching oxen. And when it had passed out of sight, he went back to the roadway and looked at the rut and found that the footprints were gone. And again he swept out his traces and went back to Juana.

She gave him the soft corncakes Apolonia had packed for them, and after a while she slept a little. But Kino sat on the ground and stared at the earth in front of him. He watched the ants moving, a little column of them near to his foot, and he put his foot in their path. Then the column climbed over his instep and continued on its way, and Kino left his foot there and watched them move over it.

The sun arose hotly. They were not near the Gulf now, and the air was dry and hot so that the brush cricked with heat and a good resinous smell came from it. And when Juana awakened, when the sun was high, Kino told her things she knew already.

"Beware of that kind of tree there," he said, pointing. "Do not touch it, for if you do and then touch your eyes, it will blind you. And beware of the tree that bleeds. See, that one over there. For if you break it the red blood will flow from it, and it is evil luck." And she nodded and smiled a little at him, for she knew these things.

"Will they follow us?" she asked. "Do you think they will try to find us?"

"They will try," said Kino. "Whoever finds us will take the pearl. Oh, they will try."

And Juana said, "Perhaps the dealers were right and the pearl has no value. Perhaps this has all been an illusion."

Kino reached into his clothes and brought out the pearl. He let the sun play on it until it burned in his eyes. "No," he said, "they would not have tried to steal it if it had been valueless."

"Do you know who attacked you? Was it the dealers?"

"I do not know," he said. "I didn't see them."

He looked into his pearl to find his vision. "When we sell it at last, I will have a rifle," he said, and he looked into the shining surface for his rifle, but he saw only a huddled dark body on the ground with shining blood dripping from its throat. And he said quickly, "We will be married in a great church." And in the pearl he saw Juana with her beaten face crawling home through the night. "Our son must learn to read," he said frantically. And there in the pearl Coyotito's face, thick and feverish from the medicine.

And Kino thrust the pearl back into his clothing, and the music of the pearl had become sinister in his ears, and it was interwoven with the music of evil.

The hot sun beat on the earth so that Kino and Juana moved into the lacy shade of the brush, and small gray birds scampered on the ground in the shade. In the heat of the day Kino relaxed and covered his eyes with his hat and wrapped his blanket about his face to keep the flies off, and he slept.

But Juana did not sleep. She sat quiet as a stone and her face was quiet. Her mouth was still swollen where Kino had struck her, and big flies buzzed around the cut on her chin. But she sat as still as a sentinel, and when Coyotito awakened she placed him on the ground in front of her and watched him wave his arms and kick his feet, and he smiled and gurgled at her until she smiled too. She picked up a little twig from the ground and tickled him, and she gave him water from the gourd she carried in her bundle.

Kino stirred in a dream, and he cried out in a guttural voice, and his hand moved in symbolic fighting. And then he moaned and sat up suddenly, his eyes wide and his nostrils flaring. He listened and heard only the cricking heat and the hiss of distance.

"What is it?" Juana asked.

"Hush," he said.

"You were dreaming."

"Perhaps." But he was restless, and when she gave him a corncake from her store he paused in his chewing to listen. He was uneasy and nervous; he glanced over his shoulder; he lifted the big knife and felt its edge. When Coyotito gurgled on the ground Kino said, "Keep him quiet."

"What is the matter?" Juana asked.

"I don't know."

He listened again, an animal light in his eyes. He stood up then, silently; and crouched low, he threaded his way through the brush toward the road. But he did not step into the road; he crept into the cover of a thorny tree and peered out along the way he had come.

And then he saw them moving along. His body stiffened and he drew down his head and peeked out from under a fallen branch. In the distance he could see three figures, two on foot and one on horseback. But he knew what they were, and a chill of fear went through him. Even in the distance he could see the two on foot moving slowly along, bent low to the ground. Here, one would pause and look at the earth, while the other joined him. They were the trackers, they could follow the trail of a bighorn sheep in the stone mountains. They were as sensitive as hounds. Here, he and Juana might have stepped out of the wheel rut, and these people from the inland, these hunters, could follow, could read a broken straw or a little tumbled pile of dust. Behind them, on a horse, was a dark man, his nose covered with a blanket, and across his saddle a rifle gleamed in the sun.

Kino lay as rigid as the tree limb. He barely breathed, and his eyes went to the place where he had swept out the track. Even the sweeping might be a message to the trackers. He knew these inland hunters. In a country where there was little game they managed to live because of their ability to hunt, and they were hunting him. They scuttled over the ground like animals and found a sign and crouched over it while the horseman waited.

The trackers whined a little, like excited dogs on a warming trail. Kino slowly drew his big knife to his hand and made it ready. He knew what he must do. If the trackers found the swept place, he must leap for the horseman, kill him quickly, and take the rifle. That was his only chance in the world. And as the three drew nearer on the road, Kino dug little pits with his sandaled toes so that he could leap without warning, so that his feet would not slip. He had only a little vision under the fallen limb.

Now Juana, back in her hidden place, heard the pad of the horse's hoofs, and Coyotito gurgled. She took him up quickly and put him under her shawl and gave him her breast and he was silent.

When the trackers came near, Kino could see only their legs and only the legs of the horse from under the fallen branch. He saw the dark horny feet of the men and their ragged white clothes, and he heard the creak of leather of the saddle and the clink of spurs. The trackers stopped at the swept place and studied it, and the horseman stopped. The horse flung his head up against the bit and the bit-roller clicked under his tongue and the horse snorted. Then the dark trackers turned and studied the horse and watched his ears.

Kino was not breathing, but his back arched a little and the muscles of his arms and legs stood out with tension and a line of sweat formed on his upper lip. For a long moment the trackers bent over the road, and then they moved on slowly, studying the ground ahead of them, and the horseman moved after them. The trackers scuttled along, stopping, looking, and hurrying on. They would be back, Kino knew. They would be circling and searching, peeping, stooping, and they would come back sooner or later to his covered track.

He slid backward and did not bother to cover his tracks. He could not; too many little signs were there, too many broken twigs and scuffed places and displaced stones. And there was a panic in Kino now, a panic of flight. The trackers would find his trail, he knew it. There was no escape, except in flight. He edged away from the road and went quickly and silently to the hidden place where Juana was. She looked up at him in question.

"Trackers," he said. "Come!"

And then a helplessness and a hopelessness swept over him, and his face went black and his eyes were sad. "Perhaps I should let them take me."

Instantly Juana was on her feet and her hand lay on his arm. "You have the pearl," she cried hoarsely. "Do you think they would take you back alive to say they had stolen it?"

His hand strayed limply to the place where the pearl was hidden under his clothes. "They will find it," he said weakly.

"Come," she said. "Come!"

And when he did not respond. "Do you think they would let me live? Do you think they would let the little one here live?"

Her goading struck into his brain; his lips snarled and his eyes were fierce again. "Come," he said. "We will go into the mountains. Maybe we can lose them in the mountains."

Frantically he gathered the gourds and the little bags that were their property. Kino carried a bundle in his left hand, but the big knife swung free in his right hand. He parted the brush for Juana and they hurried to the west, toward the high stone mountains. They trotted quickly through the tangle of the undergrowth. This was panic flight. Kino did not try to conceal his passage he trotted, kicking the stones, knocking the telltale leaves from the little trees. The high sun streamed down on the dry creaking earth so that even the vegetation ticked in protest. But ahead were the naked granite mountains, rising out of erosion rubble and standing monolithic against the sky. And Kino ran for the high place, as nearly all animals do when they are pursued.

This land was waterless, furred with the cacti which could store water and with the great-rooted brush which could reach deep into the earth for a little moisture and get along on very little. And underfoot was not soil but broken rock, split into small cubes, great slabs, but none of it water-rounded. Little tufts of sad dry grass grew between the stones, grass that had sprouted with one single rain and headed, dropped its seed, and died. Horned toads watched the family go by and turned their little pivoting dragon heads. And now and then a great jackrabbit, disturbed in his shade, bumped away and hid behind the nearest rock. The singing heat lay over this desert country, and ahead the stone mountains looked cool and welcoming.

And Kino fled. He knew what would happen. A little way along the road the trackers would become aware that they had missed the path, and they would come back, searching and judging, and in a little while they would find the place where Kino and Juana had rested. From there it would be easy for them—these little stones, the fallen leaves and the whipped branches, the scuffed places where a foot had slipped. Kino could see them in his mind, slipping along the track, whining a little with eagerness, and behind them, dark and half disinterested, the horseman with the rifle. His work would come last, for he would not take them back. Oh, the music of evil sang loud in Kino's head now, it sang with the whine of heat and with the dry ringing of snake rattles. It was not large and overwhelming now, but secret and poisonous, and the pounding of his heart gave it undertone and rhythm.

The way began to rise, and as it did the rocks grew larger. But now Kino had put a little distance between his family and the trackers. Now, on the first rise, he rested. He climbed a great boulder and looked back over the shimmering country, but he could not see his enemies, not even the tall horseman riding through the brush. Juana had squatted in the shade of the boulder. She raised her bottle of water to Coyotito's lips; his little dried tongue sucked greedily at it. She looked up at Kino when he came back; she saw him examine her ankles, cut and scratched from the stones and brush, and she covered them quickly with her skirt. Then she handed the bottle to him, but he shook his head. Her eyes were bright in her tired face. Kino moistened his cracked lips with his tongue.

"Juana," he said, "I will go on and you will hide. I will lead them into the mountains, and when they have gone past, you will go north to Loreto or to Santa Rosalia. Then, if I can escape them, I will come to you. It is the only safe way."

She looked full into his eyes for a moment. "No," she said. "We go with you."

"I can go faster alone," he said harshly. "You will put the little one in more danger if you go with me."

"No," said Juana.

"You must. It is the wise thing and it is my wish," he said.

"No," said Juana.

He looked then for weakness in her face, for fear or ir-resolution, and there was none. Her eyes were very bright. He shrugged his shoulders helplessly then, but he had taken strength from her. When they moved on it was no longer panic flight.

The country, as it rose toward the mountains, changed rapidly. Now there were long outcroppings of granite with deep crevices between, and Kino walked on bare unmark-able stone when he could and leaped from ledge to ledge. He knew that wherever the trackers lost his path they must circle and lose time before they found it again. And so he did not go straight for the mountains any more; he moved in zigzags, and sometimes he cut back to the south and left a sign and then went toward the mountains over bare stone again. And the path rose steeply now, so that he panted a little as he went.

The sun moved downward toward the bare stone teeth of the mountains, and Kino set his direction for a dark and shadowy cleft in the range. If there were any water at all, it would be there where he could see, even in the distance, a hint of foliage. And if there were any passage through the smooth stone range, it would be by this same deep cleft. It had its danger, for the trackers would think of it too, but the empty water bottle did not let that consideration enter. And as the sun lowered, Kino and Juana struggled wearily up the steep slope toward the cleft.

High in the gray stone mountains, under a frowning peak, a little spring bubbled out of a rupture in the stone. It was fed by shade-preserved snow in the summer, and now and then it died completely and bare rocks and dry algae were on its bottom. But nearly always it gushed out, cold and clean and lovely. In the times when the quick rains fell, it might become a freshet and send its column of white water crashing down the mountain cleft, but nearly always it was a lean little spring. It bubbled out into a pool and then fell a hundred feet to another pool, and this one, overflowing, dropped again, so that it continued, down and down, until it came to the rubble of the upland, and there it disappeared altogether. There wasn't much left of it then anyway, for every time it fell over an escarpment the thirsty air drank it, and it splashed from the pools to the dry vegetation. The animals from miles around came to drink from the little pools, and the wild sheep and the deer, the pumas and racoons, and the mice—all came to drink. And the birds which spent the day in the brushland came at night to the little pools that were like steps in the mountain cleft. Beside this tiny stream, wherever enough earth collected for root-hold, colonies of plants grew, wild grape and little palms, maidenhair fern, hibiscus, and tall pampas grass with feathery rods raised above the spike leaves. And in the pool lived frogs and water-skaters, and waterworms crawled on the bottom of the pool. Everything that loved water came to these few shallow places. The cats took their prey there, and strewed feathers and lapped water through their bloody teeth. The little pools were places of life because of the water, and places of killing because of the water, too.

The lowest step, where the stream collected before it tumbled down a hundred feet and disappeared into the rubbly desert, was a little platform of stone and sand. Only a pencil of water fell into the pool, but it was enough to keep the pool full and to keep the ferns green in the underhang of the cliff, and wild grape climbed the stone mountain and all manner of little plants found comfort here. The freshets had made a small sandy beach through which the pool flowed, and bright green watercress grew in the damp sand. The beach was cut and scarred and padded by the feet of animals that had come to drink and to hunt.

The sun had passed over the stone mountains when Kino and Juana struggled up the steep broken slope and came at last to the water. From this step they could look out over the sunbeaten desert to the blue Gulf in the distance. They came utterly weary to the pool, and Juana slumped to her knees and first washed Coyotito's face and then filled her bottle and gave him a drink. And the baby was weary and petulant, and he cried softly until Juana gave him her breast, and then he gurgled and clucked against her. Kino drank long and thirstily at the pool. For a moment, then, he stretched out beside the water and relaxed all his muscles and watched Juana feeding the baby, and then he got to his feet and went to the edge of the step where the water slipped over, and he searched the distance carefully. His eyes set on a point and he became rigid. Far down the slope he could see the two trackers; they were little more than dots or scurrying ants and behind them a larger ant.

Juana had turned to look at him and she saw his back stiffen.

"How far?" she asked quietly.

"They will be here by evening," said Kino. He looked up the long steep chimney of the cleft where the water came down. "We must go west," he said, and his eyes searched the stone shoulder behind the cleft. And thirty feet up on the gray shoulder he saw a series of little erosion caves. He slipped off his sandals and clambered up to them, gripping the bare stone with his toes, and he looked into the shallow caves. They were only a few feet deep, wind-hollowed scoops, but they sloped slightly downward and back. Kino crawled into the largest one and lay down and knew that he could not be seen from the outside. Quickly he went back to Juana.

"You must go up there. Perhaps they will not find us there," he said.

Without question she filled her water bottle to the top, and then Kino helped her up to the shallow cave and brought up the packages of food and passed them to her. And Juana sat in the cave entrance and watched him. She saw that he did not try to erase their tracks in the sand. Instead, he climbed up the brush cliff beside the water, clawing and tearing at the ferns and wild grape as he went. And when he had climbed a hundred feet to the next bench, he came down again. He looked carefully at the smooth rock shoulder toward the cave to see that there was no trace of passage, and last he climbed up and crept into the cave beside Juana.

"When they go up," he said, "we will slip away, down to the lowlands again. I am afraid only that the baby may cry. You must see that he does not cry."

"He will not cry," she said, and she raised the baby's face to her own and looked into his eyes and he stared solemnly back at her.

"He knows," said Juana.

Now Kino lay in the cave entrance, his chin braced on his crossed arms, and he watched the blue shadow of the mountain move out across the brushy desert below until it reached the Gulf, and the long twilight of the shadow was over the land.

The trackers were long in coming, as though they had trouble with the trail Kino had left. It was dusk when they came at last to the little pool. And all three were on foot now, for a horse could not climb the last steep slope. From above they were thin figures in the evening. The two trackers scurried about on the little beach, and they saw Kino's progress up the cliff before they drank. The man with the rifle sat down and rested himself, and the trackers squatted near him, and in the evening the points of their cigarettes glowed and receded. And then Kino could see that they were eating, and the soft murmur of their voices came to him.

Then darkness fell, deep and black in the mountain cleft. The animals that used the pool came near and smelled men there and drifted away again into the darkness.

He heard a murmur behind him. Juana was whispering, "Coyotito." She was begging him to be quiet. Kino heard the baby whimper, and he knew from the muffled sounds that Juana had covered his head with her shawl.

Down on the beach a match flared, and in its momentary light Kino saw that two of the men were sleeping, curled up like dogs, while the third watched, and he saw the glint of the rifle in the match light. And then the match died, but it left a picture on Kino's eyes. He could see it, just how each man was, two sleeping curled up and the third squatting in the sand with the rifle between his knees.

Kino moved silently back into the cave. Juana's eyes were two sparks reflecting a low star. Kino crawled quietly close to her and he put his lips near to her cheek.

"There is a way," he said.

"But they will kill you."

"If I get first to the one with the rifle," Kino said, "I must get to him first, then I will be all right. Two are sleeping."

Her hand crept out from under her shawl and gripped his arm. "They will see your white clothes in the starlight."

"No," he said. "And I must go before moonrise."

He searched for a soft word and then gave it up. "If they kill me," he said, "lie quietly. And when they are gone away, go to Loreto."

Her hand shook a little, holding his wrist.

"There is no choice," he said. "It is the only way. They will find us in the morning."

Her voice trembled a little. "Go with God," she said.

He peered closely at her and he could see her large eyes. His hand fumbled out and found the baby, and for a moment his palm lay on Coyotito's head. And then Kino raised his hand and touched Juana's creek, and she held her breath.

Against the sky in the cave entrance Juana could see that Kino was taking off his white clothes, for dirty and ragged though they were they would show up against the dark night. His own brown skin was a better protection for him. And then she saw how he hooked his amulet neck-string about the horn handle of his great knife, so that it hung down in front of him and left both hands free. He did not come back to her. For a moment his body was black in the cave entrance, crouched and silent, and then he was gone.

Juana moved to the entrance and looked out. She peered like an owl from the hole in the mountain, and the baby slept under the blanket on her back, his face turned sideways against her neck and shoulder. She could feel his warm breath against her skin, and Juana whispered her combination of prayer and magic, her Hail Marys and her ancient intercession, against the black unhuman things.

The night seemed a little less dark when she looked out, and to the east there was a lightning in the sky, down near the horizon where the moon would show. And, looking down, she could see the cigarette of the man on watch.

Kino edged like a slow lizard down the smooth rock shoulder. He had turned his neck-string so that the great knife hung down from his back and could not clash against the stone. His spread fingers gripped the mountain, and his bare toes found support through contact, and even his chest lay against the stone so that he would not slip. For any sound, a rolling pebble or a sigh, a little slip of flesh on rock, would rouse the watchers below. Any sound that was not germane to the night would make them alert. But the night was not silent; the little tree frogs that lived near the stream twittered like birds, and the high metallic ringing of the cicadas filled the mountain cleft. And Kino's own music was in his head, the music of the enemy, low and pulsing, nearly asleep. But the Song of the Family had become as fierce and sharp and feline as the snarl of a female puma. The family song was alive now and driving him down on the dark enemy. The harsh cicada seemed to take up its melody, and the twittering tree frogs called little phrases of it.

And Kino crept silently as a shadow down the smooth mountain face. One bare foot moved a few inches and the toes touched the stone and gripped, and the other foot a few inches, and then the palm of one hand a little downward, and then the other hand, until the whole body, without seeming to move, had moved. Kino's mouth was open so that even his breath would make no sound, for he knew that he was not invisible. If the watcher, sensing movement, looked at the dark place against the stone which was his body, he could see him. Kino must move so slowly he would not draw the watcher's eyes. It took him a long time to reach the bottom and to crouch behind a little dwarf palm. His heart thundered in his chest and his hands and face were wet with sweat. He crouched and took great slow long breaths to calm himself.

Only twenty feet separated him from the enemy now, and he tried to remember the ground between. Was there any stone which might trip him in his rush? He kneaded his legs against cramp and found that his muscles were jerking after their long tension. And then he looked apprehensively to the east. The moon would rise in a few moments now, and he must attack before it rose. He could see the outline of the watcher, but the sleeping men were below his vision. It was the watcher Kino must find—must find quickly and without hesitation. Silently he drew the amulet string over his shoulder and loosened the loop from the horn handle of his great knife.

He was too late, for as he rose from his crouch the silver edge of the moon slipped above the eastern horizon, and Kino sank back behind his bush.

It was an old and ragged moon, but it threw hard light and hard shadow into the mountain cleft, and now Kino could see the seated figure of the watcher on the little beach beside the pool. The watcher gazed full at the moon, and then he lighted another cigarette, and the match illumined his dark face for a moment. There could be no waiting now; when the watcher turned his head, Kino must leap. His legs were as tight as wound springs.

And then from above came a little murmuring cry. The watcher turned his head to listen and then he stood up, and one of the sleepers stirred on the ground and awakened and asked quietly, "What is it?"

"I don't know," said the watcher. "It sounded like a cry, almost like a human—like a baby."

The man who had been sleeping said, "You can't tell. Some coyote bitch with a litter. I've heard a coyote pup cry like a baby."

The sweat rolled in drops down Kino's forehead and fell into his eyes and burned them. The little cry came again and the watcher looked up the side of the hill to the dark cave.

"Coyote maybe," he said, and Kino heard the harsh click as he cocked the rifle.

"If it's a coyote, this will stop it," the watcher said as he raised the gun.

Kino was in mid-leap when the gun crashed and the barrel-flash made a picture on his eyes. The great knife swung and crunched hollowly. It bit through neck and deep into chest, and Kino was a terrible machine now. He grasped the rifle even as he wrenched free his knife. His strength and his movement and his speed were a machine. He whirled and struck the head of the seated man like a melon. The third man scrabbled away like a crab, slipped into the pool, and then he began to climb frantically, to climb up the cliff where the water penciled down. His hands and feet threshed in the tangle of the wild grapevine, and he whimpered and gibbered as he tried to get up. But Kino had become as cold and deadly as steel. Deliberately he threw the lever of the rifle, and then he raised the gun and aimed deliberately and fired. He saw his enemy tumble backward into the pool, and Kino strode to the water. In the moonlight he could see the frantic frightened eyes, and Kino aimed and fired between the eyes.

And then Kino stood uncertainly. Something was wrong, some signal was trying to get through to his brain. Tree frogs and cicadas were silent now. And then Kino's brain cleared from its red concentration and he knew the sound— the keening, moaning, rising hysterical cry from the little cave in the side of the stone mountain, the cry of death.

Everyone in La Paz remembers the return of the family; there may be some old ones who saw it, but those whose fathers and whose grandfathers told it to them remember it nevertheless. It is an event that happened to everyone. It was late in the golden afternoon when the first little boys ran hysterically in the town and spread the word that Kino and Juana were coming back. And everyone hurried to see them. The sun was settling toward the western mountains and the shadows on the ground were long. And perhaps that was what left the deep impression on those who saw them.

The two came from the rutted country road into the city, and they were not walking in single file, Kino ahead and Juana behind, as usual, but side by side. The sun was behind them and their long shadows stalked ahead, and they seemed to carry two towers of darkness with them. Kino had a rifle across his arm and Juana carried her shawl like a sack over her shoulder. And in it was a small limp heavy bundle. The shawl was crusted with dried blood, and the bundle swayed a little as she walked. Her face was hard and lined and leathery with fatigue and with the tightness with which she fought fatigue. And her wide eyes stared inward on herself. She was as remote and as removed as Heaven. Kino's lips were thin and his jaws tight, and the people say that he carried fear with him, that he was as dangerous as a rising storm. The people say that the two seemed to be removed from human experience; that they had gone through pain and had come out on the other side; that there was almost a magical protection about them. And those people who had rushed to see them crowded back and let them pass and did not speak to them.

Kino and Juana walked through the city as though it were not there. Their eyes glanced neither right nor left nor up nor down, but stared only straight ahead. Their legs moved a little jerkily, like well-made wooden dolls, and they carried pillars of black fear about them. And as they walked through the stone and plaster city brokers peered at them from barred windows and servants put one eye to a slitted gate and mothers turned the faces of their youngest children inward against their skirts. Kino and Juana strode side by side through the stone and plaster city and down among the brush houses, and the neighbors stood back and let them pass. Juan Tomás raised his hand in greeting and did not say the greeting and left his hand in the air for a moment uncertainly.

In Kino's ears the Song of the Family was as fierce as a cry. He was immune and terrible, and his song had become a battle cry. They trudged past the burned square where their house had been without even looking at it. They cleared the brush that edged the beach and picked their way down the shore toward the water. And they did not look toward Kino's broken canoe.

And when they came to the water's edge they stopped and stared out over the Gulf. And then Kino laid the rifle down, and he dug among his clothes, and then he held the great pearl in his hand. He looked into its surface and it was gray and ulcerous. Evil faces peered from it into his eyes, and he saw the light of burning. And in the surface of the pearl he saw the frantic eyes of the man in the pool. And in the surface of the pearl he saw Coyotito lying in the little cave with the top of his head shot away. And the pearl was ugly; it was gray, like a malignant growth. And Kino heard the music of the pearl, distorted and insane. Kino's hand shook a little, and he turned slowly to Juana and held the pearl out to her. She stood beside him, still holding her dead bundle over her shoulder. She looked at the pearl in his hand for a moment and then she looked into Kino's eyes and said softly, "No, you."

And Kino drew back his arm and flung the pearl with all his might. Kino and Juana watched it go, winking and glimmering under the setting sun. They saw the little splash in the distance, and they stood side by side watching the place for a long time.

And the pearl settled into the lovely green water and dropped toward the bottom. The waving branches of the algae called to it and beckoned to it. The lights on its surface were green and lovely. It settled down to the sand bottom among the fernlike plants. Above, the surface of the water was a green mirror. And the pearl lay on the floor of the sea. A crab scampering over the bottom raised a little cloud of sand, and when it settled the pearl was gone.

And the music of the pearl drifted to a whisper and disappeared.

The Red Pony

I. The Gift

AT daybreak Billy Buck emerged from the bunk-house and stood for a moment on the porch looking up at the sky. He was a broad, bandy-legged little man with a walrus mustache, with square hands, puffed and muscled on the palms. His eyes were a contemplative, watery gray and the hair which protruded from under his Stetson hat was spiky and weathered. Billy was still stuffing his shirt into his blue jeans as he stood on the porch. He unbuckled his belt and tightened it again. The belt showed, by the worn shiny places opposite each hole, the gradual increase of Billy's middle over a period of years. When he had seen to the weather, Billy cleared each nostril by holding its mate closed with his forefinger and blowing fiercely. Then he walked down to the barn, rubbing his hands together. He curried and brushed two saddle horses in the stalls, talking quietly to them all the time; and he had hardly finished when the iron triangle started ringing at the ranch house. Billy stuck the brush and currycomb together and laid them on the rail, and went up to breakfast. His action had been so deliberate and yet so wasteless of time that he came to the house while Mrs. Tiflin was still ringing the triangle. She nodded her gray head to him and withdrew into the kitchen. Billy Buck sat down on the steps, because he was a cow-hand, and it wouldn't be fitting that he should go first into the dining-room. He heard Mr. Tiflin in the house, stamping his feet into his boots.

The high jangling note of the triangle put the boy Jody in motion. He was only a little boy, ten years old, with hair like dusty yellow grass and with shy polite gray eyes, and with a mouth that worked when he thought. The triangle picked him up out of sleep. It didn't occur to him to disobey the harsh note. He never had: no one he knew ever had. He brushed the tangled hair out of his eyes and skinned his nightgown off. In a moment he was dressed—blue chambray shirt and overalls. It was late in the summer, so of course there were no shoes to bother with. In the kitchen he waited until his mother got from in front of the sink and went back to the stove. Then he washed himself and brushed back his wet hair with his fingers. His mother turned sharply on him as he left the sink. Jody looked shyly away.

"I've got to cut your hair before long," his mother said. "Breakfast's on the table. Go on in, so Billy can come."

Jody sat at the long table which was covered with white oilcloth washed through to the fabric in some places. The fried eggs lay in rows on their platter. Jody took three eggs on his plate and followed with three thick slices of crisp bacon. He carefully scraped a spot of blood from one of the egg yolks.

Billy Buck clumped in. "That won't hurt you," Billy explained. "That's only a sign the rooster leaves."

Jody's tall stern father came in then and Jody knew from the noise on the floor that he was wearing boots, but he looked under the table anyway, to make sure. His father turned off the oil lamp over the table, for plenty of morning light now came through the windows.

Jody did not ask where his father and Billy Buck were riding that day, but he wished he might go along. His father was a disciplinarian. Jody obeyed him in everything without questions of any kind. Now, Carl Tiflin sat down and reached for the egg platter.

"Got the cows ready to go, Billy?" he asked.

"In the lower corral," Billy said. "I could just as well take them in alone."

"Sure you could. But a man needs company. Besides your throat gets pretty dry." Carl Tiflin was jovial this morning.

Jody's mother put her head in the door. "What time do you think to be back, Carl?"

"I can't tell. I've got to see some men in Salinas. Might be gone till dark."

The eggs and coffee and big biscuits disappeared rapidly. Jody followed the two men out of the house. He watched them mount their horses and drive six old milk cows out of the corral and start over the hill toward Salinas. They were going to sell the old cows to the butcher.

When they had disappeared over the crown of the ridge Jody walked up the hill in back of the house. The dogs trotted around the house corner hunching their shoulders and grinning horribly with pleasure. Jody patted their heads —Doubletree Mutt with the big thick tail and yellow eyes, and Smasher, the shepherd, who had killed a coyote and lost an ear in doing it. Smasher's one good ear stood up higher than a collie's ear should. Billy Buck said that always happened. After the frenzied greeting the dogs lowered their noses to the ground in a businesslike way and went ahead, looking back now and then to make sure that the boy was coming. They walked up through the chicken yard and saw the quail eating with the chickens. Smasher chased the chickens a little to keep in practice in case there should ever be sheep to herd. Jody continued on through the large vegetable patch where the green corn was higher than his head. The cowpumpkins were green and small yet. He went on to the sagebrush line where the cold spring ran out of its pipe and fell into a round wooden tub. He leaned over and drank close to the green mossy wood where the water tasted best. Then he turned and looked back on the ranch, on the low, whitewashed house girded with red geraniums, and on the long bunkhouse by the cypress tree where Billy Buck lived alone. Jody could see the great black kettle under the cypress tree. That was where the pigs were scalded. The sun was coming over the ridge now, glaring on the whitewash of the houses and barns, making the wet grass blaze softly. Behind him, in the tall sagebrush, the birds were scampering on the ground, making a great noise among the dry leaves; the squirrels piped shrilly on the side-hills. Jody looked along at the farm buildings. He felt an uncertainty in the air, a feeling of change and of loss and of the gain of new and unfamiliar things. Over the hillside two big black buzzards sailed low to the ground and their shadows slipped smoothly and quickly ahead of them. Some animal had died in the vicinity. Jody knew it. It might be a cow or it might be the remains of a rabbit. The buzzards overlooked nothing. Jody hated them as all decent things hate them, but they could not be hurt because they made away with carrion.

After a while the boy sauntered downhill again. The

dogs had long ago given him up and gone into the brush to do things in their own way. Back through the vegetable garden he went, and he paused for a moment to smash a green muskmelon with his heel, but he was not happy about it. It was a bad thing to do, he knew perfectly well. He kicked dirt over the ruined melon to conceal it.

Back at the house his mother bent over his rough hands, inspecting his fingers and nails. It did little good to start him clean to school for too many things could happen on the way. She sighed over the black cracks on his fingers, and then gave him his books and his lunch and started him on the mile walk to school. She noticed that his mouth was working a good deal this morning.

Jody started his journey. He filled his pockets with little pieces of white quartz that lay in the road, and every so often he took a shot at a bird or at some rabbit that had stayed sunning itself in the road too long. At the cross-roads over the bridge he met two friends and the three of them walked to school together, making ridiculous strides and being rather silly. School had just opened two weeks before. There was still a spirit of revolt among the pupils.

It was four o'clock in the afternoon when Jody topped the hill and looked down on the ranch again. He looked for the saddle horses, but the corral was empty. His father was not back yet. He went slowly, then, toward the afternoon chores. At the ranch house, he found his mother sitting on the porch, mending socks.

"There's two doughnuts in the kitchen for you," she said. Jody slid to the kitchen, and returned with half of one of the doughnuts already eaten and his mouth full. His mother asked him what he had learned in school that day, but she didn't listen to his doughnut-muffled answer. She interrupted, "Jody, tonight see you fill the wood-box clear full. Last night you crossed the sticks and it wasn't only about half full. Lay the sticks flat tonight. And Jody, some of the hens are hiding eggs, or else the dogs are eating them. Look about in the grass and see if you can find any nests."

Jody, still eating, went out and did his chores. He saw the quail come down to eat with the chickens when he threw out the grain. For some reason his father was proud to have them come. He never allowed any shooting near the house for fear the quail might go away.

When the wood-box was full, Jody took his twenty-two rifle up to the cold spring at the brush line. He drank again and then aimed the gun at all manner of things, at rocks, at birds on the wing, at the big black pig kettle under the cypress tree, but he didn't shoot for he had no cartridges and wouldn't have until he was twelve. If his father had seen him aim the rifle in the direction of the house he would have put the cartridges off another year. Jody remembered this and did not point the rifle down the hill again. Two years was enough to wait for cartridges. Nearly all of his father's presents were given with reservations which hampered their value somewhat. It was good discipline.

The supper waited until dark for his father to return. When at last he came in with Billy Buck, Jody could smell the delicious brandy on their breaths. Inwardly he rejoiced, for his father sometimes talked to him when he smelled of brandy, sometimes even told things he had done in the wild days when he was a boy.

After supper, Jody sat by the fireplace and his shy polite eyes sought the room corners, and he waited for his father to tell what it was he contained, for Jody knew he had news of some sort. But he was disappointed. His father pointed a stern finger at him.

"You'd better go to bed, Jody. I'm going to need you in the morning."

That wasn't so bad. Jody liked to do the things he had to do as long as they weren't routine things. He looked at the floor and his mouth worked out a question before he spoke it. "What are we going to do in the morning, kill a pig?" he asked softly.

"Never you mind. You better get to bed."

When the door was closed behind him, Jody heard his father and Billy Buck chuckling and he knew it was a joke of some kind. And later, when he lay in bed, trying to make words out of the murmurs in the other room, he heard his father protest, "But, Ruth, I didn't give much for him."

Jody heard the hoot-owls hunting mice down by the barn, and he heard a fruit-tree limb tap-tapping against the house. A cow was lowing when he went to sleep.

When the triangle sounded in the morning, Jody dressed more quickly even than usual. In the kitchen, while he washed his face and combed back his hair, his mother addressed him irritably. "Don't you go out until you get a good breakfast in you."

He went into the dining-room and sat at the long white table. He took a steaming hotcake from the platter, arranged two fried eggs on it, covered them with another hotcake and squashed the whole thing with his fork.

His father and Billy Buck came in. Jody knew from the sound on the floor that both of them were wearing flat-heeled shoes, but he peered under the table to make sure. His father turned off the oil lamp, for the day had arrived, and he looked stern and disciplinary, but Billy Buck didn't look at Jody at all. He avoided the shy questioning eyes of the boy and soaked a whole piece of toast in his coffee.

Carl Tiflin said crossly, "You come with us after break-fast!"

Jody had trouble with his food then, for he felt a kind of doom in the air. After Billy had tilted his saucer and drained the coffee which had slopped into it, and had wiped his hands on his jeans, the two men stood up from the table and went out into the morning light together, and Jody respectfully followed a little behind them. He tried to keep his mind from running ahead, tried to keep it absolutely motionless.

His mother called, "Carl! Don't you let it keep him from school."

They marched past the cypress, where a singletree hung from a limb to butcher the pigs on, and past the black iron kettle, so it was not a pig killing. The sun shone over the hill and threw long, dark shadows of the trees and buildings. They crossed a stubble-field to shortcut to the barn. Jody's father unhooked the door and they went in. They had been walking toward the sun on the way down. The barn was black as night in contrast and warm from the hay and from the beasts. Jody's father moved over toward the one box stall. "Come here!" he ordered. Jody could begin to see things now. He looked into the box stall and then stepped back quickly.

A red pony colt was looking at him out of the stall. Its tense ears were forward and a light of disobedience was in its eyes. Its coat was rough and thick as an airdale's fur and its mane was long and tangled. Jody's throat collapsed in on itself and cut his breath short.

"He needs a good currying," his father said, "and if I ever hear of you not feeding him or leaving his stall dirty, I'll sell him off in a minute."

Jody couldn't bear to look at the pony's eyes any more. He gazed down at his hands for a moment, and he asked very shyly, "Mine?" No one answered him. He put his hand out toward the pony. Its gray nose came close, sniffing loudly, and then the lips drew back and the strong teeth closed on Jody's fingers. The pony shook its head up and down and seemed to laugh with amusement. Jody regarded his bruised fingers. "Well," he said with pride— "Well, I guess he can bite all right." The two men laughed, somewhat in relief. Carl Tiflin went out of the barn and walked up a side-hill to be by himself, for he was embarrassed, but Billy Buck stayed. It was easier to talk to Billy Buck. Jody asked again—"Mine?"

Billy became professional in tone. "Sure! That is, if you look out for him and break him right. I'll show you how. He's just a colt. You can't ride him for some time."

Jody put out his bruised hand again, and this time the red pony let his nose be rubbed. "I ought to have a carrot," Jody said. "Where'd we get him, Billy?"

"Bought him at a sheriff's auction," Billy explained. "A show went broke in Salinas and had debts. The sheriff was selling off their stuff."

The pony stretched out his nose and shook the forelock from his wild eyes. Jody stroked the nose a little. He said softly, "There isn't a—saddle?"

Billy Buck laughed. "I'd forgot. Come along."

In the harness room he lifted down a little saddle of red morocco leather. "It's just a show saddle," Billy Buck said disparagingly. "It isn't practical for the brush, but it was cheap at the sale."

Jody couldn't trust himself to look at the saddle either, and he couldn't speak at all. He brushed the shining red leather with his fingertips, and after a long time he said, "It'll look pretty on him though." He thought of the grandest and prettiest things he knew. "If he hasn't a name already, I think I'll call him Gabilan Mountains," he said.

Billy Buck knew how he felt. "It's a pretty long name. Why don't you just call him Gabilan? That means hawk. That would be a fine name for him." Billy felt glad. "If you will collect tail hair, I might be able to make a hair rope for you sometime. You could use it for a hackamore."

Jody wanted to go back to the box stall. "Could I lead him to school, do you think—to show the kids?"

But Billy shook his head. "He's not even halter-broke yet.

We had a time getting him here. Had to almost drag him. You better be starting for school though."

"I'll bring the kids to see him here this afternoon," Jody said.

Six boys came over the hill half an hour early that afternoon, running hard, their heads down, their forearms working, their breath whistling. They swept by the house and cut across the stubble-field to the barn. And then they stood self-consciously before the pony, and then they looked at Jody with eyes in which there was a new admiration and a new respect. Before today Jody had been a boy, dressed in overalls and a blue shirt—quieter than most, even suspected of being a little cowardly. And now he was different. Out of a thousand centuries they drew the ancient admiration of the footman for the horseman. They knew instinctively that a man on a horse is spiritually as well as physically bigger than a man on foot. They knew that Jody had been miraculously lifted out of equality with them, and had been placed over them. Gabilan put his head out of the stall and sniffed them.

"Why'n't you ride him?" the boys cried. "Why'n't you braid his tail with ribbons like in the fair?" "When you going to ride him?"

Jody's courage was up. He too felt the superiority of the horseman. "He's not old enough. Nobody can ride him for a long time. I'm going to train him on the long halter. Billy Buck is going to show me how."

"Well, can't we even lead him around a little?"

"He isn't even halter-broke," Jody said. He wanted to be completely alone when he took the pony out the first time. "Come and see the saddle."

They were speechless at the red morocco saddle, completely shocked out of comment. "It isn't much use in the brush," Jody explained. "It'll look pretty on him though. Maybe I'll ride bareback when I go into the brush."

"How you going to rope a cow without a saddle horn?"

"Maybe I'll get another saddle for every day. My father might want me to help him with the stock." He let them feel the red saddle, and showed them the brass chain throat-latch on the bridle and the big brass buttons at each temple where the headstall and brow band crossed. The whole thing was too wonderful. They had to go away after a little while, and each boy, in his mind, searched among his pos-sessions for a bribe worthy of offering in return for a ride on the red pony when the time should come.

Jody was glad when they had gone. He took brush and currycomb from the wall, took down the barrier of the box stall and stepped cautiously in. The pony's eyes glittered, and he edged around into kicking position. But Jody touched him on the shoulder and rubbed his high arched neck as he had always seen Billy Buck do, and he crooned, "So-o-o, boy," in a deep voice. The pony gradually relaxed his tenseness. Jody curried and brushed until a pile of dead hair lay in the stall and until the pony's coat had taken on a deep red shine. Each time he finished he thought it might have been done better. He braided the mane into a dozen little pigtails, and he braided the forelock, and then he un-did them and brushed the hair out straight again.

Jody did not hear his mother enter the barn. She was angry when she came, but when she looked in at the pony and at Jody working over him, she felt a curious pride rise up in her. "Have you forgot the wood-box?" she asked gently. "It's not far off from dark and there's not a stick of wood in the house, and the chickens aren't fed."

Jody quickly put up his tools. "I forgot, ma'am."

"Well, after this do your chores first. Then you won't forget. I expect you'll forget lots of things now if I don't keep an eye on you."

"Can I have carrots from the garden for him, ma'am?"

She had to think about that. "Oh—I guess so, if you only take the big tough ones."

"Carrots keep the coat good," he said, and again she felt the curious rush of pride.

Jody never waited for the triangle to get him out of bed after the coming of the pony. It became his habit to creep out of bed even before his mother was awake, to slip into his clothes and to go quietly down to the barn to see Gabilan. In the gray quiet mornings when the land and the brush and the houses and the trees were silver-gray and black like a photograph negative, he stole toward the barn, past the sleeping stones and the sleeping cypress tree. The turkeys, roosting in the tree out of coyotes' reach, clicked drowsily. The fields glowed with a gray frostlike light and in the dew the tracks of rabbits and of field mice stood out sharply. The good dogs came stiffly out of their little houses, hackles up and deep growls in their throats. Then they caught Jody's scent, and their stiff tails rose up and waved a greeting—Doubletree Mutt with the big thick tail, and Smasher, the incipient shepherd—then went lazily back to their warm beds.

It was a strange time and a mysterious journey, to Jody—an extension of a dream. When he first had the pony he liked to torture himself during the trip by thinking Gabilan would not be in his stall, and worse, would never have been there. And he had other delicious little self-induced pains. He thought how the rats had gnawed ragged holes in the red saddle, and how the mice had nibbled Gabilan's tail until it was stringy and thin. He usually ran the last little way to the barn. He unlatched the rusty hasp of the barn door and stepped in, and no matter how quietly he opened the door, Gabilan was always looking at him over the barrier of the box stall and Gabilan whinnied softly and stamped his front foot, and his eyes had big sparks of red fire in them like oak-wood embers.

Sometimes, if the work horses were to be used that day, Jody found Billy Buck in the barn harnessing and curry-ing. Billy stood with him and looked long at Gabilan and he told Jody a great many things about horses. He explained that they were terribly afraid for their feet, so that one must make a practice of lifting the legs and patting the hoofs and ankles to remove their terror. He told Jody how horses love conversation. He must talk to the pony all the time, and tell him the reasons for everything. Billy wasn't sure a horse could understand everything that was said to him, but it was impossible to say how much was understood. A horse never kicked up a fuss if some one he liked explained things to him. Billy could give examples, too. He had known, for instance, a horse nearly dead beat with fatigue to perk up when told it was only a little farther to his destination. And he had known a horse paralyzed with fright to come out of it when his rider told him what it was that was frightening him. While he talked in the mornings, Billy Buck cut twenty or thirty straws into neat three-inch lengths and stuck them into his hatband. Then during the whole day, if he wanted to pick his teeth or merely to chew on something, he had only to reach up for one of them.

Jody listened carefully, for he knew and the whole coun-try knew that Billy Buck was a fine hand with horses. Billy's own horse was a stringy cayuse with a hammer head, but he nearly always won the first prizes at the stock trials. Billy could rope a steer, take a double half-hitch about the horn with his riata, and dismount, and his horse would play the steer as an angler plays a fish, keeping a tight rope until the steer was down or beaten.

Every morning, after Jody had curried and brushed the

pony, he let down the barrier of the stall, and Gabilan thrust past him and raced down the barn and into the corral. Around and around he galloped, and sometimes he jumped forward and landed on stiff legs. He stood quivering, stiff ears forward, eyes rolling so that the whites showed, pretending to be frightened. At last he walked snorting to the water-trough and buried his nose in the water up to the nostrils. Jody was proud then, for he knew that was the way to judge a horse. Poor horses only touched their lips to the water, but a fine spirited beast put his whole nose and mouth under, and only left room to breathe.

Then Jody stood and watched the pony, and he saw things he had never noticed about any other horse, the sleek, sliding flank muscles and the cords of the buttocks, which flexed like a closing fist, and the shine the sun put on the red coat. Having seen horses all his life, Jody had never looked at them very closely before. But now he noticed the moving ears which gave expression and even inflection of expression to the face. The pony talked with his ears. You could tell exactly how he felt about everything by the way his ears pointed. Sometimes they were stiff and upright and sometimes lax and sagging. They went back when he was angry or fearful, and forward when he was anxious and curious and pleased; and their exact position indicated which emotion he had.

Billy Buck kept his word. In the early fall the training began. First there was the halter-breaking, and that was the hardest because it was the first thing. Jody held a carrot and coaxed and promised and pulled on the rope. The pony set his feet like a burro when he felt the strain. But before long he learned. Jody walked all over the ranch leading him. Gradually he took to dropping the rope until the pony followed him unled wherever he went.

And then came the training on the long halter. That was

slower work. Jody stood in the middle of a circle, holding
the long halter. He clucked with his tongue and the pony
started to walk in a big circle, held in by the long rope. He
clucked again to make the pony trot, and again to make him
gallop. Around and around Gabilan went thundering and
enjoying it immensely. Then he called, "Whoa," and the
pony stopped. It was not long until Gabilan was perfect at
it. But in many ways he was a bad pony. He bit Jody in the
pants and stomped on Jody's feet. Now and then his ears
went back and he aimed a tremendous kick at the boy. Every time he did one of these bad things, Gabilan settled
back and seemed to laugh to himself.

Billy Buck worked at the hair rope in the evenings before
the fireplace. Jody collected tail hair in a bag, and he sat
and watched Billy slowly constructing the rope, twisting a
few hairs to make a string and rolling two strings together
for a cord, and then braiding a number of cords to make
the rope. Billy rolled the finished rope on the floor under
his foot to make it round and hard.

The long halter work rapidly approached perfection.
Jody's father, watching the pony stop and start and trot and
gallop, was a little bothered by it.

"He's getting to be almost a trick pony," he complained.
"I don't like trick horses. It takes all the—dignity out of a
horse to make him do tricks. Why, a trick horse is kind of
like an actor—no dignity, no character of his own." And his
father said, "I guess you better be getting him used to the
saddle pretty soon."

Jody rushed for the harness-room. For some time he had
been riding the saddle on a sawhorse. He changed the stirrup length over and over, and could never get it just right.
Sometimes, mounted on the sawhorse in the harness-room,
with collars and hames and tugs hung all about him, Jody
rode out beyond the room. He carried his rifle across the

pommel. He saw the fields go flying by, and he heard the beat of the galloping hoofs.

It was a ticklish job, saddling the pony the first time. Gabilan hunched and reared and ·threw the saddle off before the cinch could be tightened. It had to be replaced again and again until at last the pony let it stay. And the cinching was difficult, too. Day by day Jody tightened the girth a little more until at last the pony didn't mind the saddle at all.

Then there was the bridle. Billy explained how to use a stick of licorice for a bit until Gabilan was used to having something in his mouth. Billy explained, "Of course we could force-break him to everything, but he wouldn't be as good a horse if we did. He'd always be a little bit afraid, and he wouldn't mind because he wanted to."

The first time the pony wore the bridle he whipped his head about and worked his tongue against the bit until the blood oozed from the corners of his mouth. He tried to rub the headstall off on the manger. His ears pivoted about and his eyes turned red with fear and with general rambunctiousness. Jody rejoiced, for he knew that only a mean-souled horse does not resent training.

And Jody trembled when he thought of the time when he would first sit in the saddle. The pony would probably throw him off. There was no disgrace in that. The disgrace would come if he did not get right up and mount again. Sometimes he dreamed that he lay in the dirt and cried and couldn't make himself mount again. The shame of the dream lasted until the middle of the day.

Gabilan was growing fast. Already he had lost the long-leggedness of the colt; his mane was getting longer and blacker. Under the constant currying and brushing his coat lay as smooth and gleaming as orange-red lacquer. Jody oiled the hoofs and kept them carefully trimmed so they would not crack.

The hair rope was nearly finished. Jody's father gave him an old pair of spurs and bent in the side bars and cut down the strap and took up the chainlets until they fitted. And then one day Carl Tiflin said:

"The pony's growing faster than I thought. I guess you can ride him by Thanksgiving. Think you can stick on?"

"I don't know," Jody said shyly. Thanksgiving was only three weeks off. He hoped it wouldn't rain, for rain would spot the red saddle.

Gabilan knew and liked Jody by now. He nickered when Jody came across the stubble-field, and in the pasture he came running when his master whistled for him. There was always a carrot for him every time.

Billy Buck gave him riding instructions over and over. "Now when you get up there, just grab tight with your knees and keep your hands away from the saddle, and if you get throwed, don't let that stop you. No matter how good a man is, there's always some horse can pitch him. You just climb up again before he gets to feeling smart about it. Pretty soon, he won't throw you no more, and pretty soon he *can't* throw you no more. That's the way to do it."

"I hope it don't rain before," Jody said.

"Why not? Don't want to get throwed in the mud?"

That was partly it, and also he was afraid that in the flurry of bucking Gabilan might slip and fall on him and break his leg or his hip. He had seen that happen to men before, had seen how they writhed on the ground like squashed bugs, and he was afraid of it.

He practiced on the sawhorse how he would hold the reins in his left hand and a hat in his right hand. If he kept his hands thus busy, he couldn't grab the horn if he felt himself going off. He didn't like to think of what would happen if he did grab the horn. Perhaps his father and Billy Buck would never speak to him again, they would be so ashamed. The news would get about and his mother would be ashamed too. And in the schoolyard—it was too awful to contemplate.

He began putting his weight in a stirrup when Gabilan was saddled, but he didn't throw his leg over the pony's back. That was forbidden until Thanksgiving.

Every afternoon he put the red saddle on the pony and cinched it tight. The pony was learning already to fill his stomach out unnaturally large while the cinching was going on, and then to let it down when the straps were fixed. Sometimes Jody led him up to the brush line and let him drink from the round green tub, and sometimes he led him up through the stubble-field to the hilltop from which it was possible to see the white town of Salinas and the geometric fields of the great valley, and the oak trees clipped by the sheep. Now and then they broke through the brush and came to little cleared circles so hedged in that the world was gone and only the sky and the circle of brush were left from the old life. Gabilan liked these trips and showed it by keeping his head very high and by quivering his nostrils with interest. When the two came back from an expedition they smelled of the sweet sage they had forced through.

Time dragged on toward Thanksgiving, but winter came fast. The clouds swept down and hung all day over the land and brushed the hilltops, and the winds blew shrilly at night. All day the dry oak leaves drifted down from the trees until they covered the ground, and yet the trees were unchanged.

Jody had wished it might not rain before Thanksgiving, but it did. The brown earth turned dark and the trees glistened. The cut ends of the stubble turned black with mildew; the haystacks grayed from exposure to the damp, and on the roofs the moss, which had been all summer as gray as lizards, turned a brilliant yellow-green. During the week of rain, Jody kept the pony in the box stall out of the dampness, except for a little time after school when he took him out for exercise and to drink at the water-trough in the upper corral. Not once did Gabilan get wet.

The wet weather continued until little new grass appeared. Jody walked to school dressed in a slicker and short rubber boots. At length one morning the sun came out brightly. Jody, at his work in the box stall, said to Billy Buck, "Maybe I'll leave Gabilan in the corral when I go to school today."

"Be good for him to be out in the sun," Billy assured him. "No animal likes to be cooped up too long. Your father and me are going back on the hill to clean the leaves out of the spring." Billy nodded and picked his teeth with one of his little straws.

"If the rain comes, though—" Jody suggested.

"Not likely to rain today. She's rained herself out." Billy pulled up his sleeves and snapped his arm bands. "If it comes on to rain—why a little rain don't hurt a horse."

"Well, if it does come to rain, you put him in, will you, Billy? I'm scared he might get cold so I couldn't ride him when the time comes."

"Oh sure! I'll watch out for him if we get back in time. But it won't rain today."

And so Jody, when he went to school, left Gabilan standing out in the corral.

Billy Buck wasn't wrong about many things. He couldn't be. But he was wrong about the weather that day, for a little after noon the clouds pushed over the hills and the rain began to pour down. Jody heard it start on the schoolhouse roof. He considered holding up one finger for permission to go to the outhouse and, once outside, running for home to put the pony in. Punishment would be prompt both at school and at home. He gave it up and took ease from Billy's assurance that rain couldn't hurt a horse. When school was finally out, he hurried home through the dark rain. The banks at the sides of the road spouted little jets of muddy water. The rain slanted and swirled under a cold and gusty wind. Jody dog-trotted home, slopping through the gravelly mud of the road.

From the top of the ridge he could see Gabilan standing miserably in the corral. The red coat was almost black, and streaked with water. He stood head down with his rump to the rain and wind. Jody arrived running and threw open the barn door and led the wet pony in by his forelock. Then he found a gunny sack and rubbed the soaked hair and rubbed the legs and ankles. Gabilan stood patiently, but he trembled in gusts like the wind.

When he had dried the pony as well as he could, Jody went up to the house and brought hot water down to the barn and soaked the grain in it. Gabilan was not very hungry. He nibbled at the hot mash, but he was not very much interested in it, and he still shivered now and then. A little steam rose from his damp back.

It was almost dark when Billy Buck and Carl Tiflin came home. "When the rain started we put up at Ben Herche's place, and the rain never let up all afternoon," Carl Tiflin explained. Jody looked reproachfully at Billy Buck and Billy felt guilty.

"You said it wouldn't rain," Jody accused him.

Billy looked away. "It's hard to tell, this time of year," he said, but his excuse was lame. He had no right to be fallible, and he knew it.

"The pony got wet, got soaked through."

"Did you dry him off?"

"I rubbed him with a sack and I gave him hot grain."

Billy nodded in agreement.

"Do you think he'll take cold, Billy?"

"A little rain never hurt anything," Billy assured him.

Jody's father joined the conversation then and lectured the boy a little. "A horse," he said, "isn't any lap-dog kind of thing." Carl Tiflin hated weakness and sickness, and he held a violent contempt for helplessness.

Jody's mother put a platter of steaks on the table and boiled potatoes and boiled squash, which clouded the room with their steam. They sat down to eat. Carl Tiflin still grumbled about weakness put into animals and men by too much coddling.

Billy Buck felt bad about his mistake. "Did you blanket him?" he asked.

"No. I couldn't find any blanket. I laid some sacks over his back."

"We'll go down and cover him up after we eat, then." Billy felt better about it then. When Jody's father had gone in to the fire and his mother was washing dishes, Billy found and lighted a lantern. He and Jody walked through the mud to the barn. The barn was dark and warm and sweet. The horses still muched their evening hay. "You hold the lantern!" Billy ordered. And he felt the pony's legs and tested the heat of the flanks. He put his cheek against the pony's gray muzzle and then he rolled up the eyelids to look at the eyeballs and he lifted the lips to see the gums, and he put his fingers inside his ears. "He don't seem so chipper," Billy said. "I'll give him a rubdown."

Then Billy found a sack and rubbed the pony's legs violently and he rubbed the chest and the withers. Gabilan was strangely spiritless. He submitted patiently to the rubbing. At last Billy brought an old cotton comforter from the saddle-room, and threw it over the pony's back and tied it at neck and chest with string.

"Now he'll be all right in the morning," Billy said.

Jody's mother looked up when he got back to the house. "You're late up from bed," she said. She held his chin in her hard hand and brushed the tangled hair out of his eyes and she said, "Don't worry about the pony. He'll be all right. Billy's as good as any horse doctor in the country."

Jody hadn't known she could see his worry. He pulled gently away from her and knelt down in front of the fireplace until it burned his stomach. He scorched himself through and then went in to bed, but it was a hard thing to go to sleep. He awakened after what seemed a long time. The room was dark but there was a grayness in the window like that which precedes the dawn. He got up and found his overalls and searched for the legs, and then the clock in the other room struck two. He laid his clothes down and got back into bed. It was broad daylight when he awakened again. For the first time he had slept through the ringing of the triangle. He leaped up, flung on his clothes and went out of the door still buttoning his shirt. His mother looked after him for a moment and then went quietly back to her work. Her eyes were brooding and kind. Now and then her mouth smiled a little but without changing her eyes at all.

Jody ran on toward the barn. Halfway there he heard the sound he dreaded, the hollow rasping cough of a horse. He broke into a sprint then. In the barn he found Billy Buck with the pony. Billy was rubbing its legs with his strong thick hands. He looked up and smiled gaily. "He just took a little cold," Billy said. "We'll have him out of it in a couple of days."

Jody looked at the pony's face. The eyes were half closed and the lids thick and dry. In the eye corners a crust of hard mucus stuck. Gabilan's ears hung loosely sideways and his head was low. Jody put out his hand, but the pony did not move close to it. He coughed again and his whole body constricted with the effort. A little stream of thin fluid ran from his nostrils.

Jody looked back at Billy Buck. "He's awful sick, Billy."

"Just a little cold, like I said," Billy insisted. "You go get some breakfast and then go back to school. I'll take care of him."

"But you might have to do something else. You might leave him."

"No, I won't. I won't leave him at all. Tomorrow's Saturday. Then you can stay with him all day." Billy had failed again, and he felt badly about it. He had to cure the pony now.

Jody walked up to the house and took his place listlessly at the table. The eggs and bacon were cold and greasy, but he didn't notice it. He ate his usual amount. He didn't even ask to stay home from school. His mother pushed his hair back when she took his plate. "Billy'll take care of the pony," she assured him.

He moped through the whole day at school. He couldn't answer any questions nor read any words. He couldn't even tell anyone the pony was sick, for that might make him sicker. And when school was finally out he started home in dread. He walked slowly and let the other boys leave him. He wished he might continue walking and never arrive at the ranch.

Billy was in the barn, as he had promised, and the pony was worse. His eyes were almost closed now, and his breath whistled shrilly past an obstruction in his nose. A film covered that part of the eyes that was visible at all. It was doubtful whether the pony could see any more. Now and then he snorted, to clear his nose, and by the action seemed to plug it tighter. Jody looked dispiritedly at the pony's coat. The hair lay rough and unkempt and seemed to have lost all of its old luster. Billy stood quietly beside the stall. Jody hated to ask, but he had to know.

"Billy, is he—is he going to get well?"

Billy put his fingers between the bars under the pony's jaw and felt about. "Feel here," he said and he guided Jody's fingers to a large lump under the jaw. "When that gets bigger, I'll open it up and then he'll get better."

Jody looked quickly away, for he had heard about that lump. "What is the matter with him?"

Billy didn't want to answer, but he had to. He couldn't be wrong three times. "Strangles," he said shortly, "but don't you worry about that. I'll pull him out of it. I've seen them get well when they were worse than Gabilan is. I'm going to steam him now. You can help."

"Yes," Jody said miserably. He followed Billy into the grain room and watched him make the steaming bag ready. It was a long canvas nose bag with straps to go over a horse's ears. Billy filled it one-third full of bran and then he added a couple of handfuls of dried hops. On top of the dry substance he poured a little carbolic acid and a little turpentine. "I'll be mixing it all up while you run to the house for a kettle of boiling water," Billy said.

When Jody came back with the steaming kettle, Billy buckled the straps over Gabilan's head and fitted the bag tightly around his nose. Then through a little hole in the side of the bag he poured the boiling water on the mixture. The pony started away as a cloud of strong steam rose up, but then the soothing fumes crept through his nose and into his lungs, and the sharp steam began to clear out the nasal passages. He breathed loudly. His legs trembled in an ague, and his eyes closed against the biting cloud. Billy poured in more water and kept the steam rising for fifteen minutes. At last he set down the kettle and took the bag from Gabilan's nose. The pony looked better. He breathed freely, and his eyes were open wider than they had been.

"See how good it makes him feel," Billy said. "Now we'll wrap him up in the blanket again. Maybe he'll be nearly well by morning."

"I'll stay with him tonight," Jody suggested.

"No. Don't you do it. I'll bring my blankets down here

and put them in the hay. You can stay tomorrow and steam him if he needs it."

The evening was falling when they went to the house for their supper. Jody didn't even realize that some one else had fed the chickens and filled the wood-box. He walked up past the house to the dark brushline and took a drink of water from the tub. The spring water was so cold that it stung his mouth and drove a shiver through him. The sky above the hills was still light. He saw a hawk flying so high that it caught the sun on its breast and shone like a spark. Two blackbirds were driving him down the sky, glittering as they attacked their enemy. In the west, the clouds were moving in to rain again.

Jody's father didn't speak at all while the family ate supper, but after Billy Buck had taken his blankets and gone to sleep in the barn, Carl Tiflin built a high fire in the fireplace and told stories. He told about the wild man who ran naked through the country and had a tail and ears like a horse, and he told about the rabbit-cats of Moro Cojo that hopped into the trees for birds. He revived the famous Maxwell brothers who found a vein of gold and hid the traces of it so carefully that they could never find it again.

Jody sat with his chin in his hands; his mouth worked nervously, and his father gradually became aware that he wasn't listening very carefully. "Isn't that funny?" he asked.

Jody laughed politely and said, "Yes, sir." His father was angry and hurt, then. He didn't tell any more stories. After a while, Jody took a lantern and went down to the barn. Billy Buck was asleep in the hay, and, except that his breath rasped a little in his lungs, the pony seemed to be much better. Jody stayed a little while, running his fingers over the red rough coat, and then he took up the lantern and went back to the house. When he was in bed, his mother came into the room.

"Have you enough covers on? It's getting winter."

"Yes, ma'am."

"Well, get some rest tonight." She hesitated to go out, stood uncertainly. "The pony will be all right," she said.

Jody was tired. He went to sleep quickly and didn't awaken until dawn. The triangle sounded, and Billy Buck came up from the barn before Jody could get out of the house.

"How is he?" Jody demanded.

Billy always wolfed his breakfast. "Pretty good. I'm going to open that lump this morning. Then he'll be better maybe."

After breakfast, Billy got out his best knife, one with a needle point. He whetted the shining blade a long time on a little carborundum stone. He tried the point and the blade again and again on his calloused thumb-ball, and at last he tried it on his upper lip.

On the way to the barn, Jody noticed how the young grass was up and how the stubble was melting day by day into the new green crop of volunteer. It was a cold sunny morning.

As soon as he saw the pony, Jody knew he was worse. His eyes were closed and sealed shut with dried mucus. His head hung so low that his nose almost touched the straw of his bed. There was a little groan in each breath, a deep-seated, patient groan.

Billy lifted the weak head and made a quick slash with the knife. Jody saw the yellow pus run out. He held up the head while Billy swabbed out the wound with weak carbolic acid salve.

"Now he'll feel better," Billy assured him. "That yellow poison is what makes him sick."

Jody looked unbelieving at Billy Buck. "He's awful sick."

Billy thought a long time what to say. He nearly tossed off a careless assurance, but he saved himself in time. "Yes, he's pretty sick," he said at last. "I've seen worse ones get well. If he doesn't get pneumonia, we'll pull him through. You stay with him. If he gets worse, you can come and get me."

For a long time after Billy went away, Jody stood beside the pony, stroking him behind the ears. The pony didn't flip his head the way he had done when he was well. The groaning in his breathing was becoming more hollow.

Doubletree Mutt looked into the barn, his big tail waving provocatively, and Jody was so incensed at his health that he found a hard black clod on the floor and deliberately threw it. Doubletree Mutt went yelping away to nurse a bruised paw.

In the middle of the morning, Billy Buck came back and made another steam bag. Jody watched to see whether the pony improved this time as he had before. His breathing eased a little, but he did not raise his head.

The Saturday dragged on. Late in the afternoon Jody went to the house and brought his bedding down and made up a place to sleep in the hay. He didn't ask permission. He knew from the way his mother looked at him that she would let him do almost anything. That night he left a lantern burning on a wire over the box stall. Billy had told him to rub the pony's legs every little while.

At nine o'clock the wind sprang up and howled around the barn. And in spite of his worry, Jody grew sleepy. He got into his blankets and went to sleep, but the breathy groans of the pony sounded in his dreams. And in his sleep he heard a crashing noise which went on and on until it awakened him. The wind was rushing through the barn. He sprang up and looked down the lane of stalls. The barn door had blown open, and the pony was gone.

He caught the lantern and ran outside into the gale, and he saw Gabilan weakly shambling away into the darkness, head down, legs working slowly and mechanically. When

Jody ran up and caught him by the forelock, he allowed himself to be led back and put into his stall. His groans were louder, and a fierce whistling came from his nose. Jody didn't sleep any more then. The hissing of the pony's breath grew louder and sharper.

He was glad when Billy Buck came in at dawn. Billy looked for a time at the pony as though he had never seen him before. He felt the ears and flanks. "Jody," he said, "I've got to do something you won't want to see. You run up to the house for a while."

Jody grabbed him fiercely by the forearm. "You're not going to shoot him?"

Billy patted his hand. "No. I'm going to open a little hole in his windpipe so he can breathe. His nose is filled up. When he gets well, we'll put a little brass button in the hole for him to breathe through."

Jody couldn't have gone away if he had wanted to. It was awful to see the red hide cut, but infinitely more terrible to know it was being cut and not to see it. "I'll stay right here," he said bitterly. "You sure you got to?"

"Yes, I'm sure. If you stay, you can hold his head. If it doesn't make you sick, that is."

The fine knife came out again and was whetted again just as carefully as it had been the first time. Jody held the pony's head up and the throat taut, while Billy felt up and down for the right place. Jody sobbed once as the bright knife point disappeared into the throat. The pony plunged weakly away and then stood still, trembling violently. The blood ran thickly out and up the knife and across Billy's hand and into his shirtsleeve. The sure square hand sawed out a round hole in the flesh, and the breath came bursting out of the hole, throwing a fine spray of blood. With the rush of oxygen, the pony took a sudden strength. He lashed out with his hind feet and tried to rear, but Jody held his head down while Billy mopped the new wound with carbolic salve. It was a good job. The blood stopped flowing and the air puffed out the hole and sucked it in regularly with a little bubbling noise.

The rain brought in by the night wind began to fall on the barn roof. Then the triangle rang for breakfast. "You go up and eat while I wait," Billy said. "We've got to keep this hole from plugging up."

Jody walked slowly out of the barn. He was too dispirited to tell Billy how the barn door had blown open and let the pony out. He emerged into the wet gray morning and sloshed up to the house, taking a perverse pleasure in splashing through all the puddles. His mother fed him and put dry clothes on. She didn't question him. She seemed to know he couldn't answer questions. But when he was ready to go back to the barn she brought him a pan of steaming meal. "Give him this," she said.

But Jody did not take the pan. He said, "He won't eat anything," and ran out of the house. At the barn, Billy showed him how to fix a ball of cotton on a stick, with which to swab out the breathing hole when it became clogged with mucus.

Jody's father walked into the barn and stood with them in front of the stall. At length he turned to the boy. "Hadn't you better come with me? I'm going to drive over the hill." Jody shook his head. "You better come on, out of this," his father insisted.

Billy turned on him angrily. "Let him alone. It's his pony, isn't it?"

Carl Tiflin walked away without saying another word. His feelings were badly hurt.

All morning Jody kept the wound open and the air passing in and out freely. At noon the pony lay wearily down on his side and stretched his nose out.

Billy came back. "If you're going to stay with him tonight, you better take a little nap," he said. Jody went ab-

sently out of the barn. The sky had cleared to a hard thin blue. Everywhere the birds were busy with worms that had come to the damp surface of the ground.

Jody walked to the brush line and sat on the edge of the mossy tub. He looked down at the house and at the old bunkhouse and at the dark cypress tree. The place was familiar, but curiously changed. It wasn't itself any more, but a frame for things that were happening. A cold wind blew out of the east now, signifying that the rain was over for a little while. At his feet Jody could see the little arms of new weeds spreading out over the ground. In the mud about the spring were thousands of quail tracks.

Doubletree Mutt came sideways and embarrassed up through the vegetable patch, and Jody, remembering how he had thrown the clod, put his arm about the dog's neck and kissed him on his wide black nose. Doubletree Mutt sat still, as though he knew some solemn thing was happening. His big tail slapped the ground gravely. Jody pulled a swollen tick out of Mutt's neck and popped it dead between his thumb-nails. It was a nasty thing. He washed his hands in the cold spring water.

Except for the steady swish of the wind, the farm was very quiet. Jody knew his mother wouldn't mind if he didn't go in to eat his lunch. After a little while he went slowly back to the barn. Mutt crept into his own little house and whined softly to himself for a long time.

Billy Buck stood up from the box and surrendered the cotton swab. The pony still lay on his side and the wound in his throat bellowsed in and out. When Jody saw how dry and dead the hair looked, he knew at last that there was no hope for the pony. He had seen the dead hair before on dogs and on cows, and it was a sure sign. He sat heavily on the box and let down the barrier of the box stall. For a long time he kept his eyes on the moving wound, and at last he dozed, and the afternoon passed quickly. Just before dark his mother brought a deep dish of stew and left it for him and went away. Jody ate a little of it, and, when it was dark, he set the lantern on the floor by the pony's head so he could watch the wound and keep it open. And he dozed again until the night chill awakened him. The wind was blowing fiercely, bringing the north cold with it. Jody brought a blanket from his bed in the hay and wrapped himself in it. Gabilan's breathing was quiet at last; the hole in his throat moved gently. The owls flew through the hayloft, shrieking and looking for mice. Jody put his hands down on his head and slept. In his sleep he was aware that the wind had increased. He heard it slamming about the barn.

It was daylight when he awakened. The barn door had swung open. The pony was gone. He sprang up and ran out into the morning light.

The pony's tracks were plain enough, dragging through the frostlike dew on the young grass, tired tracks with little lines between them where the hoofs had dragged. They headed for the brush line halfway up the ridge. Jody broke into a run and followed them. The sun shone on the sharp white quartz that stuck through the ground here and there. As he followed the plain trail, a shadow cut across in front of him. He looked up and saw a high circle of black buzzards, and the slowly revolving circle dropped lower and lower. The solemn birds soon disappeared over the ridge. Jody ran faster then, forced on by panic and rage. The trail entered the brush at last and followed a winding route among the tall sagebrushes.

At the top of the ridge Jody was winded. He paused, puffing noisily. The blood pounded in his ears. Then he saw what he was looking for. Below, in one of the little clearings in the brush lay the red pony. In the distance, Jody could see the legs moving slowly and convulsively. And in a circle around him stood the buzzards, waiting for the moment of death they know so well.

Jody leaped forward and plunged down the hill. The wet ground muffled his steps and the brush hid him. When he arrived, it was all over. The first buzzard sat on the pony's head and its beak had just risen dripping with dark eye fluid. Jody plunged into the circle like a cat. The black brotherhood arose in a cloud, but the big one on the pony's head was too late. As it hopped along to take off, Jody caught its wing tip and pulled it down. It was nearly as big as he was. The free wing crashed into his face with the force of a club, but he hung on. The claws fastened on his leg and the wing elbows battered his head on either side. Jody groped blindly with his free hand. His fingers found the neck of the struggling bird. The red eyes looked into his face, calm and fearless and fierce; the naked head turned from side to side. Then the beak opened and vomited a stream of putrefied fluid. Jody brought up his knees and fell on the great bird. He held the neck to the ground with one hand while his other found a piece of sharp white quartz. The first blow broke the beak sideways and black blood spurted from the twisted, leathery mouth corners. He struck again and missed. The red fearless eyes still looked at him, impersonal and unafraid and detached. He struck again and again, until the buzzard lay dead, until its head was a red pulp. He was still beating the dead bird when Billy Buck pulled him off and held him tightly to calm his shaking.

Carl Tiflin wiped the blood from the boy's face with a red bandana. Jody was limp and quiet now. His father moved the buzzard with his toe. "Jody," he explained, "the buzzard didn't kill the pony. Don't you know that?"

"I know it," Jody said wearily.

It was Billy Buck who was angry. He had lifted Jody in his arms, and had turned to carry him home. But he turned back on Carl Tiflin. " 'Course he knows it," Billy said furiously. "Jesus Christ! man, can't you see how he'd feel about it?"

2. The Great Mountains

IN the humming heat of a midsummer afternoon the little boy Jody listlessly looked about the ranch for something to do. He had been to the barn, had thrown rocks at the swallows' nests under the eaves until every one of the little mud houses broke open and dropped its lining of straw and dirty feathers. Then at the ranch house he baited a rat trap with stale cheese and set it where Doubletree Mutt, that good big dog, would get his nose snapped. Jody was not moved by an impulse of cruelty; he was bored with the long hot afternoon. Doubletree Mutt put his stupid nose in the trap and got it smacked, and shrieked with agony and limped away with blood on his nostrils. No matter where he was hurt, Mutt limped. It was just a way he had. Once when he was young, Mutt got caught in a coyote trap, and always after that he limped, even when he was scolded.

When Mutt yelped, Jody's mother called from inside the house, "Jody! Stop torturing that dog and find something to do."

Jody felt mean then, so he threw a rock at Mutt. Then he took his slingshot from the porch and walked up toward the brush line to try to kill a bird. It was a good slingshot, with store-bought rubbers, but while Jody had often shot at birds, he had never hit one. He walked up through the vegetable patch, kicking his bare toes into the dust. And on the way he found the perfect slingshot stone, round and slightly flattened and heavy enough to carry through the air. He fitted it into the leather pouch of his weapon and proceeded to the brush line. His eyes narrowed, his mouth worked strenuously; for the first time that afternoon he was intent. In the shade of the sagebrush the little birds were working, scratching in the leaves, flying restlessly a few feet and scratching again. Jody pulled back the rubbers of the sling and advanced cautiously. One little thrush paused and looked at him and crouched, ready to fly. Jody sidled nearer, moving one foot slowly after the other. When he was twenty feet away, he carefully raised the sling and aimed. The stone whizzed; the thrush started up and flew right into it. And down the little bird went with a broken head. Jody ran to it and picked it up.

"Well, I got you," he said.

The bird looked much smaller dead than it had alive. Jody felt a little mean pain in his stomach, so he took out his pocket-knife and cut off the bird's head. Then he disemboweled it, and took off its wings; and finally he threw all the pieces into the brush. He didn't care about the bird, or

its life, but he knew what older people would say if they had
seen him kill it; he was ashamed because of their potential
opinion. He decided to forget the whole thing as quickly as
he could, and never to mention it.

The hills were dry at this season, and the wild grass was
golden, but where the spring-pipe filled the round tub and
the tub spilled over, there lay a stretch of fine green grass,
deep and sweet and moist. Jody drank from the mossy tub
and washed the bird's blood from his hands in cold water.
Then he lay on his back in the grass and looked up at the
dumpling summer clouds. By closing one eye and destroy-
ing perspective he brought them down within reach so that
he could put up his fingers and stroke them. He helped the
gentle wind push them down the sky; it seemed to him that
they went faster for his help. One fat white cloud he helped
clear to the mountain rims and pressed it firmly over, out of
sight. Jody wondered what it was seeing, then. He sat up
the better to look at the great mountains where they went
piling back, growing darker and more savage until they
finished with one jagged ridge, high up against the west.
Curious secret mountains; he thought of the little he knew
about them.

"What's on the other side?" he asked his father once.

"More mountains, I guess. Why?"

"And on the other side of them?"

"More mountains. Why?"

"More mountains on and on?"

"Well, no. At last you come to the ocean."

"But what's in the mountains?"

"Just cliffs and brush and rocks and dryness."

"Were you ever there?"

"No."

"Has anybody ever been there?"

"A few people, I guess. It's dangerous, with cliffs and
things. Why, I've read there's more unexplored country in

the mountains of Monterey County than any place in the United States." His father seemed proud that this should be so.

"And at last the ocean?"

"At last the ocean."

"But," the boy insisted, "but in between? No one knows?"

"Oh, a few people do, I guess. But there's nothing there to get. And not much water. Just rocks and cliffs and grease-wood. Why?"

"It would be good to go."

"What for? There's nothing there."

Jody knew something was there, something very wonderful because it wasn't known, something secret and mysterious. He could feel within himself that this was so. He said to his mother, "Do you know what's in the big mountains?"

She looked at him and then back at the ferocious range, and she said, "Only the bear, I guess."

"What bear?"

"Why the one that went over the mountain to see what he could see."

Jody questioned Billy Buck, the ranch-hand, about the possibility of ancient cities lost in the mountains, but Billy agreed with Jody's father.

"It ain't likely," Billy said. "There'd be nothing to eat unless a kind of people that can eat rocks live there."

That was all the information Jody ever got, and it made the mountains dear to him, and terrible. He thought often of the miles of ridge after ridge until at last there was the sea. When the peaks were pink in the morning they invited him among them: and when the sun had gone over the edge in the evening and the mountains were a purple-like despair, then Jody was afraid of them; then they were so impersonal and aloof that their very imperturbability was a threat.

Now he turned his head toward the mountains of the east,

the Gabilans, and they were jolly mountains, with hill ranches in their creases, and with pine trees growing on the crests. People lived there, and battles had been fought against the Mexicans on the slopes. He looked back for an instant at the Great Ones and shivered a little at the contrast. The foothill cup of the home ranch below him was sunny and safe. The house gleamed with white light and the barn was brown and warm. The red cows on the farther hill ate their way slowly toward the north. Even the dark cypress tree by the bunkhouse was usual and safe. The chickens scratched about in the dust of the farmyard with quick waltzing steps.

Then a moving figure caught Jody's eye. A man walked slowly over the brow of the hill, on the road from Salinas, and he was headed toward the house. Jody stood up and moved down toward the house too, for if someone was coming, he wanted to be there to see. By the time the boy had got to the house the walking man was only halfway down the road, a lean man, very straight in the shoulders. Jody could tell he was old only because his heels struck the ground with hard jerks. As he approached nearer, Jody saw that he was dressed in blue jeans and in a coat of the same material. He wore clodhopper shoes and an old flat-brimmed Stetson hat. Over his shoulder he carried a gunny sack, lumpy and full. In a few moments he had trudged close enough so that his face could be seen. And his face was as dark as dried beef. A mustache, blue-white against the dark skin, hovered over his mouth, and his hair was white, too, where it showed at his neck. The skin of his face had shrunk back against the skull until it defined bone, not flesh, and made the nose and chin seem sharp and fragile. The eyes were large and deep and dark, with eyelids stretched tightly over them. Irises and pupils were one, and very black, but the eyeballs were brown. There were no wrinkles in the face at all. This old man wore a blue denim coat buttoned to the throat with brass buttons, as all men do who wear no shirts. Out of the sleeves came strong bony wrists and hands gnarled and knotted and hard as peach branches. The nails were flat and blunt and shiny.

The old man drew close to the gate and swung down his sack when he confronted Jody. His lips fluttered a little and a soft impersonal voice came from between them. "Do you live here?"

Jody was embarrassed. He turned and looked at the house, and he turned back and looked toward the barn where his father and Billy Buck were. "Yes," he said, when no help came from either direction.

"I have come back," the old man said. "I am Gitano, and I have come back."

Jody could not take all this responsibility. He turned abruptly, and ran into the house for help, and the screen door banged after him. His mother was in the kitchen poking out the clogged holes of a colander with a hairpin, and biting her lower lip with concentration.

"It's an old man," Jody cried excitedly. "It's an old *paisano* man, and he says he's come back."

His mother put down the colander and stuck the hairpin behind the sink board. "What's the matter now?" she asked patiently.

"It's an old man outside. Come on out."

"Well, what does he want?" She untied the strings of her apron and smoothed her hair with her fingers.

"I don't know. He came walking."

His mother smoothed down her dress and went out, and Jody followed her. Gitano had not moved.

"Yes?" Mrs. Tiflin asked.

Gitano took off his old black hat and held it with both hands in front of him. He repeated, "I am Gitano, and I have come back.

"Come back? Back where?"

Gitano's whole straight body leaned forward a little. His right hand described the circle of the hills, the sloping fields and the mountains, and ended at his hat again. "Back to the rancho. I was born here, and my father, too."

"Here?" she demanded. "This isn't an old place."

"No, there," he said, pointing to the western ridge. "On the other side there, in a house that is gone."

At last she understood. "The old 'dobe that's washed almost away, you mean?"

"Yes, *señora*. When the rancho broke up they put no more lime on the 'dobe, and the rains washed it down."

Jody's mother was silent for a little, and curious homesick thoughts ran through her mind, but quickly she cleared them out. "And what do you want here now, Gitano?"

"I will stay here," he said quietly, "until I die."

"But we don't need an extra man here."

"I cannot work hard any more, *señora*. I can milk a cow, feed chickens, cut a little wood; no more. I will stay here." He indicated the sack on the ground beside him. "Here are my things."

She turned to Jody. "Run down to the barn and call your father."

Jody dashed away, and he returned with Carl Tiflin and Billy Buck behind him. The old man was standing as he had been, but he was resting now. His whole body had sagged into a timeless repose.

"What is it?" Carl Tiflin asked. "What's Jody so excited about?"

Mrs. Tiflin motioned to the old man. "He wants to stay here. He wants to do a little work and stay here."

"Well, we can't have him. We don't need any more men. He's too old. Billy does everything we need."

They had been talking over him as though he did not

exist, and now, suddenly, they both hesitated and looked at Gitano and were embarrassed.

He cleared his throat. "I am too old to work. I come back where I was born."

"You weren't born here," Carl said sharply.

"No. In the 'dobe house over the hill. It was all one rancho before you came."

"In the mud house that's all melted down?"

"Yes. I and my father. I will stay here now on the rancho."

"I tell you you won't stay," Carl said angrily. "I don't need an old man. This isn't a big ranch. I can't afford food and doctor bills for an old man. You must have relatives and friends. Go to them. It is like begging to come to strangers."

"I was born here," Gitano said patiently and inflexibly.

Carl Tiflin didn't like to be cruel, but he felt he must. "You can eat here tonight," he said. "You can sleep in the little room of the old bunkhouse. We'll give you your breakfast in the morning, and then you'll have to go along. Go to your friends. Don't come to die with strangers."

Gitano put on his black hat and stooped for the sack. "Here are my things," he said.

Carl turned away. "Come on, Billy, we'll finish down at the barn. Jody, show him the little room in the bunkhouse."

He and Billy turned back toward the barn. Mrs. Tiflin went into the house, saying over her shoulder, "I'll send some blankets down."

Gitano looked questioningly at Jody. "I'll show you where it is," Jody said.

There was a cot with a shuck mattress, an apple box holding a tin lantern, and a backless rocking-chair in the little room of the bunkhouse. Gitano laid his sack carefully on the floor and sat down on the bed. Jody stood shyly in the room, hesitating to go. At last he said,

"Did you come out of the big mountains?"

Gitano shook his head slowly. "No, I worked down the Salinas Valley."

The afternoon thought would not let Jody go. "Did you ever go into the big mountains back there?"

The old dark eyes grew fixed, and their light turned inward on the years that were living in Gitano's head. "Once —when I was a little boy. I went with my father."

"Way back, clear into the mountains?"

"Yes."

"What was there?" Jody cried. "Did you see any people or any houses?"

"No."

"Well, what was there?"

Gitano's eyes remained inward. A little wrinkled strain came between his brows.

"What did you see in there?" Jody repeated.

"I don't know," Gitano said. "I don't remember."

"Was it terrible and dry?"

"I don't remember."

In his excitement, Jody had lost his shyness. "Don't you remember anything about it?"

Gitano's mouth opened for a word, and remained open while his brain sought the word. "I think it was quiet—I think it was nice."

Gitano's eyes seemed to have found something back in the years, for they grew soft and a little smile seemed to come and go in them.

"Didn't you ever go back in the mountains again?" Jody insisted.

"No."

"Didn't you ever want to?"

But now Gitano's face became impatient. "No," he said in a tone that told Jody he didn't want to talk about it any more. The boy was held by a curious fascination. He didn't want to go away from Gitano. His shyness returned.

"Would you like to come down to the barn and see the stock?" he asked.

Gitano stood up and put on his hat and prepared to follow.

It was almost evening now. They stood near the watering trough while the horses sauntered in from the hillsides for an evening drink. Gitano rested his big twisted hands on the top rail of the fence. Five horses came down and drank, and then stood about, nibbling at the dirt or rubbing their sides against the polished wood of the fence. Long after they had finished drinking an old horse appeared over the brow of the hill and came painfully down. It had long yellow teeth; its hoofs were flat and sharp as spades, and its ribs and hipbones jutted out under its skin. It hobbled up to the trough and drank water with a loud sucking noise.

"That's old Easter," Jody explained. "That's the first horse my father ever had. He's thirty years old." He looked up into Gitano's old eyes for some response.

"No good any more," Gitano said.

Jody's father and Billy Buck came out of the barn and walked over.

"Too old to work," Gitano repeated. "Just eats and pretty soon dies."

Carl Tiflin caught the last words. He hated his brutality toward old Gitano, and so he became brutal again.

"It's a shame not to shoot Easter," he said. "It'd save him a lot of pains and rheumatism." He looked secretly at Gitano, to see whether he noticed the parallel, but the big bony hands did not move, nor did the dark eyes turn from the horse. "Old things ought to be put out of their misery," Jody's father went on. "One shot, a big noise, one big pain in the head maybe, and that's all. That's better than stiffness and sore teeth."

Billy Buck broke in. "They got a right to rest after they worked all of their life. Maybe they like to just walk around."

Carl had been looking steadily at the skinny horse. "You can't imagine now what Easter used to look like," he said softly. "High neck, deep chest, fine barrel. He could jump a five-bar gate in stride. I won a flat race on him when I was fifteen years old. I could of got two hundred dollars for him any time. You wouldn't think how pretty he was." He checked himself, for he hated softness. "But he ought to be shot now," he said.

"He's got a right to rest," Billy Buck insisted.

Jody's father had a humorous thought. He turned to Gitano. "If ham and eggs grew on a side-hill I'd turn you out to pasture too," he said. "But I can't afford to pasture you in my kitchen."

He laughed to Billy Buck about it as they went on toward the house. "Be a good thing for all of us if ham and eggs grew on the side-hills."

Jody knew how his father was probing for a place to hurt

in Gitano. He had been probed often. His father knew every place in the boy where a word would fester.

"He's only talking," Jody said. "He didn't mean it about shooting Easter. He likes Easter. That was the first horse he ever owned."

The sun sank behind the high mountains as they stood there, and the ranch was hushed. Gitano seemed to be more at home in the evening. He made a curious sharp sound with his lips and stretched one of his hands over the fence. Old Easter moved stiffly to him, and Gitano rubbed the lean neck under the mane.

"You like him?" Jody asked softly.

"Yes—but he's no damn good."

The triangle sounded at the ranch house. "That's supper," Jody cried. "Come on up to supper."

As they walked up toward the house Jody noticed again that Gitano's body was as straight as that of a young man. Only by a jerkiness in his movements and by the scuffling of his heels could it be seen that he was old.

The turkeys were flying heavily into the lower branches of the cypress tree by the bunkhouse. A fat sleek ranch cat walked across the road carrying a rat so large that its tail dragged on the ground. The quail on the side-hills were still sounding the clear water call.

Jody and Gitano came to the back steps and Mrs. Tiflin looked out through the screen door at them.

"Come running, Jody. Come in to supper, Gitano."

Carl and Billy Buck had started to eat at the long oilcloth-covered table. Jody slipped into his chair without moving it, but Gitano stood holding his hat until Carl looked up and said, "Sit down, sit down. You might as well get your belly full before you go on." Carl was afraid he might relent and let the old man stay, and so he continued to remind himself that this couldn't be.

Gitano laid his hat on the floor and diffidently sat down. He wouldn't reach for food. Carl had to pass it to him. "Here, fill yourself up." Gitano ate very slowly, cutting tiny pieces of meat and arranging little pats of mashed potato on his plate.

The situation would not stop worrying Carl Tiflin. "Haven't you got any relatives in this part of the country?" he asked.

Gitano answered with some pride, "My brother-in-law is in Monterey. I have cousins there, too."

"Well, you can go and live there, then."

"I was born here," Gitano said in gentle rebuke.

Jody's mother came in from the kitchen, carrying a large bowl of tapioca pudding.

Carl chuckled to her, "Did I tell you what I said to him? I said if ham and eggs grew on the side-hills I'd put him out to pasture, like old Easter."

Gitano stared unmoved at his plate.

"It's too bad he can't stay," said Mrs. Tiflin.

"Now don't you start anything," Carl said crossly.

When they had finished eating, Carl and Billy Buck and Jody went into the living-room to sit for a while, but Gitano, without a word of farewell or thanks, walked through the kitchen and out the back door. Jody sat and secretly watched his father. He knew how mean his father felt.

"This country's full of these old *paisanos*," Carl said to Billy Buck.

"They're damn good men," Billy defended them. "They can work older than white men. I saw one of them a hundred and five years old, and he could still ride a horse. You don't see any white men as old as Gitano walking twenty or thirty miles."

"Oh, they're tough, all right," Carl agreed. "Say, are you standing up for him too? Listen, Billy," he explained, "I'm having a hard enough time keeping this ranch out of the Bank of Italy without taking on anybody else to feed. You know that, Billy."

"Sure, I know," said Billy. "If you was rich, it'd be different."

"That's right, and it isn't like he didn't have relatives to go to. A brother-in-law and cousins right in Monterey. Why should I worry about him?"

Jody sat quietly listening, and he seemed to hear Gitano's gentle voice and its unanswerable, "But I was born here." Gitano was mysterious like the mountains. There were ranges back as far as you could see, but behind the last range piled up against the sky there was a great unknown country. And Gitano was an old man, until you got to the dull dark eyes. And in behind them was some unknown thing. He didn't ever say enough to let you guess what was inside, under the eyes. Jody felt himself irresistibly drawn toward the bunkhouse. He slipped from his chair while his father was talking and he went out the door without making a sound.

The night was very dark and far-off noises carried in clearly. The hamebells of a wood team sounded from way over the hill on the county road. Jody picked his way across the dark yard. He could see a light through the window of the little room of the bunkhouse. Because the night was secret he walked quietly up to the window and peered in. Gitano sat in the rocking-chair and his back was toward the window. His right arm moved slowly back and forth in front of him. Jody pushed the door open and walked in. Gitano jerked upright and, seizing a piece of deerskin, he tried to throw it over the thing in his lap, but the skin slipped away. Jody stood overwhelmed by the thing in Gitano's hand, a lean and lovely rapier with a golden basket hilt. The blade was like a thin ray of dark light. The hilt was pierced and intricately carved.

"What is it?" Jody demanded.

Gitano only looked at him with resentful eyes, and he picked up the fallen deerskin and firmly wrapped the beautiful blade in it.

Jody put out his hand. "Can't I see it?"

Gitano's eyes smoldered angrily and he shook his head.

"Where'd you get it? Where'd it come from?"

Now Gitano regarded him profoundly, as though he pondered. "I got it from my father."

"Well, where'd he get it?"

Gitano looked down at the long deerskin parcel in his hand. "I don't know."

"Didn't he ever tell you?"

"No."

"What do you do with it?"

Gitano looked slightly surprised. "Nothing. I just keep it."

"Can't I see it again?"

The old man slowly unwrapped the shining blade and let the lamplight slip along it for a moment. Then he wrapped it up again. "You go now. I want to go to bed." He blew out the lamp almost before Jody had closed the door.

As he went back toward the house, Jody knew one thing more sharply than he had ever known anything. He must never tell anyone about the rapier. It would be a dreadful thing to tell anyone about it, for it would destroy some fragile structure of truth. It was a truth that might be shattered by division.

On the way across the dark yard Jody passed Billy Buck.

"They're wondering where you are," Billy said.

Jody slipped into the living-room, and his father turned to him. "Where have you been?"

"I just went out to see if I caught any rats in my new trap."

"It's time you went to bed," his father said.

Jody was first at the breakfast table in the morning. Then his father came in, and last, Billy Buck. Mrs. Tiflin looked in from the kitchen.

"Where's the old man, Billy?" he asked.

"I guess he's out walking," Billy said. "I looked in his room and he wasn't there."

"Maybe he started early to Monterey," said Carl. "It's a long walk."

"No," Billy explained. "His sack is in the little room."

After breakfast Jody walked down to the bunkhouse. Flies were flashing about in the sunshine. The ranch seemed especially quiet this morning. When he was sure no one was watching him, Jody went into the little room, and looked into Gitano's sack. An extra pair of long cotton underwear was there, an extra pair of jeans and three pairs of worn socks. Nothing else was in the sack. A sharp loneliness fell on Jody. He walked slowly back toward the house. His father stood on the porch talking to Mrs. Tiflin.

"I guess old Easter's dead at last," he said. "I didn't see him come down to water with the other horses."

In the middle of the morning Jess Taylor from the ridge ranch rode down.

"You didn't sell that old gray crowbait of yours, did you, Carl?"

"No of course not. Why?"

"Well," Jess said. "I was out this morning early, and I saw a funny thing. I saw an old man on an old horse, no saddle, only a piece of rope for a bridle. He wasn't on the road at all. He was cutting right up straight through the brush. I think he had a gun. At least I saw something shine in his hand."

"That's old Gitano," Carl Tiflin said. "I'll see if any of my guns are missing." He stepped into the house for a second. "Nope, all here. Which way was he heading, Jess?"

"Well, that's the funny thing. He was heading straight back into the mountains."

Carl laughed. "They never get too old to steal," he said. "I guess he just stole old Easter."

"Want to go after him, Carl?"

"Hell no, just save me burying that horse. I wonder where he got the gun. I wonder what he wants back there."

Jody walked up through the vegetable patch, toward the brush line. He looked searchingly at the towering mountains—ridge after ridge after ridge until at last there was the ocean. For a moment he thought he could see a black speck crawling up the farthest ridge. Jody thought of the rapier and of Gitano. And he thought of the great mountains. A longing caressed him, and it was so sharp that he wanted to cry to get it out of his breast. He lay down in the green grass near the round tub at the brush line. He covered his eyes with his crossed arms and lay there a long time, and he was full of a nameless sorrow.

3. The Promise

IN a mid-afternoon of spring, the little boy Jody walked martially along the brush-lined road toward his home ranch. Banging his knee against the golden lard bucket he used for school lunch, he contrived a good bass drum, while his tongue fluttered sharply against his teeth to fill in snare drums and occasional trumpets. Some time back the other members of the squad that walked so smartly from the school had turned into the various little canyons and taken the wagon roads to their own home ranches. Now Jody marched seemingly alone, with high-lifted knees and pounding feet; but behind him there was a phantom army with great flags and swords, silent but deadly.

The afternoon was green and gold with spring. Underneath the spread branches of the oaks the plants grew pale and tall, and on the hills the feed was smooth and thick. The sagebrushes shone with new silver leaves and the oaks wore hoods of golden green. Over the hills there hung such a green odor that the horses on the flats galloped madly, and then stopped, wondering; lambs, and even old sheep jumped in the air unexpectedly and landed on stiff legs, and went on eating; young clumsy calves butted their heads together and drew back and butted again.

As the gray and silent army marched past, led by Jody, the animals stopped their feeding and their play and watched it go by. Suddenly Jody stopped. The gray army halted, bewildered and nervous. Jody went down on his knees. The army stood in long uneasy ranks for a moment, and then, with a soft sigh of sorrow, rose up in a faint gray mist and disappeared. Jody had seen the thorny crown of a hornytoad moving under the dust of the road. His grimy hand went out and grasped the spiked halo and held firmly while the little beast struggled. Then Jody turned the horny-toad over, exposing its pale gold stomach. With a gentle forefinger he stroked the throat and chest until the horny-toad relaxed, until its eyes closed and it lay languorous and asleep.

Jody opened his lunch pail and deposited the first game inside. He moved on now, his knees bent slightly, his shoulders crouched; his bare feet were wise and silent. In his right hand there was a long gray rifle. The brush along the road stirred restively under a new and unexpected population of gray tigers and gray bears. The hunting was very good, for by the time Jody reached the fork of the road where the mail box stood on a post, he had captured two more horny-toads, four little grass lizards, a blue snake, sixteen yellow-winged grasshoppers and a brown damp newt from under a rock. This assortment scrabbled unhappily against the tin of the lunch bucket.

At the road fork the rifle evaporated and the tigers and bears melted from the hillsides. Even the moist and uncomfortable creatures in the lunch pail ceased to exist, for the little red metal flag was up on the mail box, signifying that some postal matter was inside. Jody set his pail on the ground and opened the letter box. There was a Montgomery Ward catalog and a copy of the *Salinas Weekly Journal*. He slammed the box, picked up his lunch pail and trotted over the ridge and down into the cup of the ranch. Past the barn he ran, and past the used-up haystack and the bunkhouse and the cypress tree. He banged through the front screen door of the ranch house calling, "Ma'am, ma'am, there's a catalog."

Mrs. Tiflin was in the kitchen spooning clabbered milk into a cotton bag. She put down her work and rinsed her hands under the tap. "Here in the kitchen, Jody. Here I am."

He ran in and clattered his lunch pail on the sink. "Here it is. Can I open the catalog, ma'am?"

Mrs. Tiflin took up the spoon again and went back to her cottage cheese. "Don't lose it, Jody. Your father will want to see it." She scraped the last of the milk into the bag. "Oh, Jody, your father wants to see you before you go to your chores." She waved a cruising fly from the cheese bag.

Jody closed the new catalog in alarm. "Ma'am?"

"Why don't you ever listen? I say your father wants to see you."

The boy laid the catalog gently on the sink board. "Do you—is it something I did?"

Mrs. Tiflin laughed. "Always a bad conscience. What did you do?"

"Nothing, ma'am," he said lamely. But he couldn't remember, and besides it was impossible to know what action might later be construed as a crime.

His mother hung the full bag on a nail where it could drip into the sink. "He just said he wanted to see you when you got home. He's somewhere down by the barn."

Jody turned and went out the back door. Hearing his mother open the lunch pail and then gasp with rage, a memory stabbed him and he trotted away toward the barn, conscientiously not hearing the angry voice that called him from the house.

Carl Tiflin and Billy Buck, the ranch-hand, stood against the lower pasture fence. Each man rested one foot on the lowest bar and both elbows on the top bar. They were talking slowly and aimlessly. In the pasture half a dozen horses nibbled contentedly at the sweet grass. The mare, Nellie, stood backed up against the gate, rubbing her buttocks on the heavy post.

Jody sidled uneasily near. He dragged one foot to give an impression of great innocence and nonchalance. When he arrived beside the men he put one foot on the lowest fence rail, rested his elbows on the second bar and looked into the pasture too.

The two men glanced sideways at him.

"I wanted to see you," Carl said in the stern tone he reserved for children and animals.

"Yes, sir," said Jody guiltily.

"Billy, here, says you took good care of the pony before it died."

No punishment was in the air. Jody grew bolder. "Yes, sir, I did."

"Billy says you have a good patient hand with horses."

Jody felt a sudden warm friendliness for the ranch-hand.

Billy put in, "He trained that pony as good as anybody I ever seen."

Then Carl Tiflin came gradually to the point. "If you could have another horse would you work for it?"

Jody shivered. "Yes, sir."

"Well, look here, then. Billy says the best way for you to be a good hand with horses is to raise a colt."

"It's the *only* good way," Billy interrupted.

"Now, look here, Jody," continued Carl. "Jess Taylor, up to the ridge ranch, has a fair stallion, but it'll cost five dollars. I'll put up the money, but you'll have to work it out all summer. Will you do that?"

Jody felt that his insides were shriveling. "Yes, sir," he said softly.

"And no complaining? And no forgetting when you're told to do something?"

"Yes, sir."

"Well, all right, then. Tomorrow morning you take Nellie up to the ridge ranch and get her bred. You'll have to take care of her, too, till she throws the colt."

"Yes, sir."

"You better get to the chickens and the wood now."

Jody slid away. In passing behind Billy Buck he very nearly put out his hand to touch the blue-jeaned legs. His shoulders swayed a little with maturity and importance.

He went to his work with unprecedented seriousness. This night he did not dump the can of grain to the chickens so that they had to leap over each other and struggle to get it. No, he spread the wheat so far and so carefully that the hens couldn't find some of it at all. And in the house, after listening to his mother's despair over boys who filled their lunch pails with slimy, suffocated reptiles, and bugs, he promised never to do it again. Indeed, Jody felt that all such foolishness was lost in the past. He was far too grown up ever to put horny-toads in his lunch pail any more. He carried in so much wood and built such a high structure with it that his mother walked in fear of an avalanche of oak. When he was done, when he had gathered eggs that had remained hidden for weeks, Jody walked down again past the cypress tree, and past the bunkhouse toward the pasture. A fat warty toad that looked out at him from under the watering trough had no emotional effect on him at all.

Carl Tiflin and Billy Buck were not in sight, but from a metallic ringing on the other side of the barn Jody knew that Billy Buck was just starting to milk a cow.

The other horses were eating toward the upper end of the pasture, but Nellie continued to rub herself nervously against the post. Jody walked slowly near, saying, "So, girl, so-o, Nellie." The mare's ears went back naughtily and her lips drew away from her yellow teeth. She turned her head around; her eyes were glazed and mad. Jody climbed to the top of the fence and hung his feet over and looked paternally down on the mare.

The evening hovered while he sat there. Bats and night-hawks flicked about. Billy Buck, walking toward the house carrying a full milk bucket, saw Jody and stopped. "It's a long time to wait," he said gently. "You'll get awful tired waiting."

"No, I won't, Billy. How long will it be?"

"Nearly a year."

"Well, I won't get tired."

The triangle at the house rang stridently. Jody climbed down from the fence and walked to supper beside Billy Buck. He even put out his hand and took hold of the milk bucket to help carry it.

The next morning after breakfast Carl Tiflin folded a five-dollar bill in a piece of newspaper and pinned the package in the bib pocket of Jody's overalls. Billy Buck haltered the mare Nellie and led her out of the pasture.

"Be careful now," he warned. "Hold her up short here so she can't bite you. She's crazy as a coot."

Jody took hold of the halter leather itself and started up the hill toward the ridge ranch with Nellie skittering and jerking behind him. In the pasturage along the road the wild oat heads were just clearing their scabbards. The warm morning sun shone on Jody's back so sweetly that he was forced to take a serious stiff-legged hop now and then in spite of his maturity. On the fences the shiny blackbirds with red epaulets clicked their dry call. The meadowlarks sang like water, and the wild doves, concealed among the bursting leaves of the oaks, made a sound of restrained grieving. In the fields the rabbits sat sunning themselves, with only their forked ears showing above the grass heads.

After an hour of steady uphill walking, Jody turned into a narrow road that led up a steeper hill to the ridge ranch. He could see the red roof of the barn sticking up above the oak trees, and he could hear a dog barking unemotionally near the house.

Suddenly Nellie jerked back and nearly freed herself. From the direction of the barn Jody heard a shrill whistling scream and a splintering of wood, and then a man's voice shouting. Nellie reared and whinnied. When Jody held to the halter rope she ran at him with bared teeth. He dropped his hold and scuttled out of the way, into the brush. The high scream came from the oaks again, and Nellie answered it. With hoofs battering the ground the stallion appeared and charged down the hill trailing a broken halter rope. His eyes glittered feverishly. His stiff, erected nostrils were as red as flame. His black, sleek hide shone in the sunlight. The stallion came on so fast that he couldn't stop when he reached the mare. Nellie's ears went back; she whirled and kicked at him as he went by. The stallion spun around and reared. He struck the mare with his front hoof, and while she staggered under the blow, his teeth raked her neck and drew an ooze of blood.

Instantly Nellie's mood changed. She became coquettishly feminine. She nibbled his arched neck with her lips. She edged around and rubbed her shoulder against his shoulder. Jody stood half-hidden in the brush and watched. He heard the step of a horse behind him, but before he could turn, a hand caught him by the overall straps and lifted him off the ground. Jess Taylor sat the boy behind him on the horse.

"You might have got killed," he said. "Sundog's a mean devil sometimes. He busted his rope and went right through a gate."

Jody sat quietly, but in a moment he cried, "He'll hurt her, he'll kill her. Get him away!"

Jess chuckled. "She'll be all right. Maybe you'd better climb off and go up to the house for a little. You could get maybe a piece of pie up there."

But Jody shook his head. "She's mine, and the colt's going to be mine. I'm going to raise it up."

Jess nodded. "Yes, that's a good thing. Carl has good sense sometimes."

In a little while the danger was over. Jess lifted Jody down and then caught the stallion by its broken halter rope. And he rode ahead, while Jody followed, leading Nellie.

It was only after he had unpinned and handed over the five dollars; and after he had eaten two pieces of pie, that Jody started for home again. And Nellie followed docilely after him. She was so quiet that Jody climbed on a stump and rode her most of the way home.

The five dollars his father had advanced reduced Jody to peonage for the whole late spring and summer. When the hay was cut he drove a rake. He led the horse that pulled on the Jackson-fork tackle, and when the baler came he drove the circling horse that put pressure on the bales. In addition, Carl Tiflin taught him to milk and put a cow under his care, so that a new chore was added night and morning.

The bay mare Nellie quickly grew complacent. As she walked about the yellowing hillsides or worked at easy tasks, her lips were curled in a perpetual fatuous smile. She moved slowly, with the calm importance of an empress. When she was put to a team, she pulled steadily and unemotionally. Jody went to see her every day. He studied her with critical eyes and saw no change whatever.

One afternoon Billy Buck leaned the many-tined manure

fork against the barn wall. He loosened his belt and tucked in his shirt-tail and tightened the belt again. He picked one of the little straws from his hatband and put it in the corner of his mouth. Jody, who was helping Doubletree Mutt, the big serious dog, to dig out a gopher, straightened up as the ranch-hand sauntered out of the barn.

"Let's go up and have a look at Nellie," Billy suggested.

Instantly Jody fell into step with him. Doubletree Mutt watched them over his shoulder; then he dug furiously, growled, sounded little sharp yelps to indicate that the gopher was practically caught. When he looked over his shoulder again, and saw that neither Jody nor Billy was interested, he climbed reluctantly out of the hole and followed them up the hill.

The wild oats were ripening. Every head bent sharply under its load of grain, and the grass was dry enough so that it made a swishing sound as Jody and Billy stepped through it. Halfway up the hill they could see Nellie and the iron-gray gelding, Pete, nibbling the heads from the wild oats. When they approached, Nellie looked at them and backed her ears and bobbed her head up and down rebelliously. Billy walked to her and put his hand under her mane and patted her neck, until her ears came forward again and she nibbled delicately at his shirt.

Jody asked, "Do you think she's really going to have a colt?"

Billy rolled the lids back from the mare's eyes with his thumb and forefinger. He felt the lower lip and fingered the black, leathery teats. "I wouldn't be surprised," he said.

"Well, she isn't changed at all. It's three months gone."

Billy rubbed the mare's flat forehead with his knuckle while she grunted with pleasure. "I told you you'd get tired waiting. It'll be five months more before you can even see a sign, and it'll be at least eight months more before she throws the colt, about next January."

Jody sighed deeply. "It's a long time, isn't it?"

"And then it'll be about two years more before you can ride."

Jody cried out in despair, "I'll be grown up."

"Yep, you'll be an old man," said Billy.

"What color do you think the colt'll be?"

"Why, you can't ever tell. The stud is black and the dam is bay. Colt might be black or bay or gray or dappled. You can't tell. Sometimes a black dam might have a white colt."

"Well, I hope it's black, and a stallion."

"If it's a stallion, we'll have to geld it. Your father wouldn't let you have a stallion."

"Maybe he would," Jody said. "I could train him not to be mean."

Billy pursed his lips, and the little straw that had been in the corner of his mouth rolled down to the center. "You can't ever trust a stallion," he said critically. "They're mostly fighting and making trouble. Sometimes when they're feeling funny they won't work. They make the mares uneasy and kick hell out of the geldings. Your father wouldn't let you keep a stallion."

Nellie sauntered away, nibbling the drying grass. Jody skinned the grain from a grass stem and threw the handful into the air, so that each pointed, feathered seed sailed out like a dart. "Tell me how it'll be, Billy. Is it like when the cows have calves?"

"Just about. Mares are a little more sensitive. Sometimes you have to be there to help the mare. And sometimes if it's wrong, you have to—" he paused.

"Have to what, Billy?"

"Have to tear the colt to pieces to get it out, or the mare'll die."

"But it won't be that way this time, will it, Billy?"

"Oh, no, Nellie's thrown good colts."

"Can I be there, Billy? Will you be certain to call me? It's my colt."

"Sure, I'll call you. Of course I will."

"Tell me how it'll be."

"Why, you've seen the cows calving. It's almost the same. The mare starts groaning and stretching, and then, if it's a good right birth, the head and forefeet come out, and the front hoofs kick a hole just the way the calves do. And the colt starts to breathe. It's good to be there, 'cause if its feet aren't right maybe he can't break the sac, and then he might smother."

Jody whipped his leg with a bunch of grass. "We'll have to be there, then, won't we?"

"Oh, we'll be there, all right."

They turned and walked slowly down the hill toward the barn. Jody was tortured with a thing he had to say, although he didn't want to. "Billy," he began miserably, "Billy, you won't let anything happen to the colt, will you?"

And Billy knew he was thinking of the red pony, Gabilan, and of how it died of strangles. Billy knew he had been infallible before that, and now he was capable of failure. This knowledge made Billy much less sure of himself than he had been. "I can't tell," he said roughly. "All sorts of things might happen, and they wouldn't be my fault. I can't do everything." He felt badly about his lost prestige, and so he said, meanly, "I'll do everything I know, but I won't promise anything. Nellie's a good mare. She's thrown good colts before. She ought to this time." And he walked away from Jody and went into the saddle-room beside the barn, for his feelings were hurt.

Jody traveled often to the brush line behind the house. A rusty iron pipe ran a thin stream of spring water into an old green tub. Where the water spilled over and sank into the ground there was a patch of perpetually green grass. Even when the hills were brown and baked in the summer that little patch was green. The water whined softly into the trough all the year round. This place had grown to be a center-point for Jody. When he had been punished the cool green grass and the singing water soothed him. When he had been mean the biting acid of meanness left him at the brush line. When he sat in the grass and listened to the purling stream, the barriers set up in his mind by the stern day went down to ruin.

On the other hand, the black cypress tree by the bunkhouse was as repulsive as the water-tub was dear; for to this tree all the pigs came, sooner or later, to be slaughtered. Pig killing was fascinating, with the screaming and the blood, but it made Jody's heart beat so fast that it hurt him. After the pigs were scalded in the big iron tripod kettle and their skins were scraped and white, Jody had to go to the water-tub to sit in the grass until his heart grew quiet. The water-tub and the black cypress were opposites and enemies.

When Billy left him and walked angrily away, Jody turned up toward the house. He thought of Nellie as he walked, and of the little colt. Then suddenly he saw that he was under the black cypress, under the very singletree where the pigs were hung. He brushed his dry-grass hair off his forehead and hurried on. It seemed to him an unlucky thing to be thinking of his colt in the very slaughter place, especially after what Billy had said. To counteract any evil result of that bad conjunction he walked quickly past the ranch house, through the chicken yard, through the vegetable patch, until he came at last to the brushline.

He sat down in the green grass. The trilling water sounded in his ears. He looked over the farm buildings and across at the round hills, rich and yellow with grain. He could see Nellie feeding on the slope. As usual the water place eliminated time and distance. Jody saw a black, long-legged colt, butting against Nellie's flanks, demanding milk. And then he saw himself breaking a large colt to halter. All in a few moments the colt grew to be a magnificent animal, deep of chest, with a neck as high and arched as a sea-horse's neck, with a tail that tongued and rippled like black flame. This horse was terrible to everyone but Jody. In the schoolyard the boys begged rides, and Jody smilingly agreed. But no sooner were they mounted than the black demon pitched them off. Why, that was his name, Black Demon! For a moment the trilling water and the grass and the sunshine came back, and then . . .

Sometimes in the night the ranch people, safe in their beds, heard a roar of hoofs go by. They said, "It's Jody, on Demon. He's helping out the sheriff again." And then . . .

The golden dust filled the air in the arena at the Salinas Rodeo. The announcer called the roping contests. When Jody rode the black horse to the starting chute the other contestants shrugged and gave up first place, for it was well known that Jody and Demon could rope and throw and tie a steer a great deal quicker than any roping team of two men could. Jody was not a boy any more, and Demon was not a horse. The two together were one glorious individual. And then . . .

The President wrote a letter and asked them to help catch a bandit in Washington. Jody settled himself comfortably in the grass. The little stream of water whined into the mossy tub.

The year passed slowly on. Time after time Jody gave up his colt for lost. No change had taken place in Nellie. Carl Tiflin still drove her to a light cart, and she pulled on a hay rake and worked the Jackson-ford tackle when the hay was being put into the barn.

The summer passed, and the warm bright autumn. And then the frantic morning winds began to twist along the ground, and a chill came into the air, and the poison oak turned red. One morning in September, when he had finished his breakfast, Jody's mother called him into the kitchen. She was pouring boiling water into a bucket full of dry midlings and stirring the materials to a steaming paste.

"Yes, ma'am?" Jody asked.

"Watch how I do it. You'll have to do it after this every other morning."

"Well, what is it?"

"Why, it's warm mash for Nellie. It'll keep her in good shape."

Jody rubbed his forehead with a knuckle. "Is she all right?" he asked timidly.

Mrs. Tiflin put down the kettle and stirred the mash with a wooden paddle. "Of course she's all right, only you've got to take better care of her from now on. Here, take this breakfast out to her!"

Jody seized the bucket and ran, down past the bunkhouse, past the barn, with the heavy bucket banging against his knees. He found Nellie playing with the water in the trough, pushing waves and tossing her head so that the water slopped out on the ground.

Jody climbed the fence and set the bucket of steaming mash beside her. Then he stepped back to look at her. And she was changed. Her stomach was swollen. When she moved, her feet touched the ground gently. She buried her nose in the bucket and gobbled the hot breakfast. And when she had finished and had pushed the bucket around the ground with her nose a little, she stepped quietly over to Jody and rubbed her cheek against him.

Billy Buck came out of the saddle-room and walked over. "Starts fast when it starts, doesn't it?"

"Did it come all at once?"

"Oh, no, you just stopped looking for a while." He pulled her head around toward Jody. "She's goin' to be nice, too. See how nice her eyes are! Some mares get mean, but when they turn nice, they just love everything." Nellie slipped her head under Billy's arm and rubbed her neck up and down between his arm and his side. "You better treat her awful nice now," Billy said.

"How long will it be?" Jody demanded breathlessly.

The man counted in whispers on his fingers. "About three months," he said aloud. "You can't tell exactly. Sometimes it's eleven months to the day, but it might be two weeks early, or a month late, without hurting anything."

Jody looked hard at the ground. "Billy," he began nervously, "Billy, you'll call me when it's getting born, won't you? You'll let me be there, won't you?"

Billy bit the tip of Nellie's ear with his front teeth. "Carl says he wants you to start right at the start. That's the only way to learn. Nobody can tell you anything. Like my old man did with me about the saddle blanket. He was a government packer when I was your size, and I helped him some. One day I left a wrinkle in my saddle blanket and made a saddle-sore. My old man didn't give me hell at all. But the next morning he saddled me up with a forty-pound stock saddle. I had to lead my horse and carry that saddle over a whole damn mountain in the sun. It darn near killed me, but I never left no wrinkles in a blanket again. I couldn't. I never in my life since then put on a blanket but I felt that saddle on my back."

Jody reached up a hand and took hold of Nellie's mane. "You'll tell me what to do about everything, won't you? I guess you know everything about horses, don't you?"

Billy laughed. "Why I'm half horse myself, you see," he said. "My ma died when I was born, and being my old man was a government packer in the mountains, and no cows around most of the time, why he just gave me mostly mare's milk." He continued seriously, "And horses know that. Don't you know it, Nellie?"

The mare turned her head and looked full into his eyes for a moment, and this is a thing horses practically never do. Billy was proud and sure of himself now. He boasted a little. "I'll see you get a good colt. I'll start you right. And if you do like I say, you'll have the best horse in the county."

That made Jody feel warm and proud, too; so proud that when he went back to the house he bowed his legs and swayed his shoulders as horsemen do. And he whispered, "Whoa, you Black Demon, you! Steady down there and keep your feet on the ground."

The winter fell sharply. A few preliminary gusty showers, and then a strong steady rain. The hills lost their straw color and blackened under the water, and the winter streams scrambled noisily down the canyons. The mushrooms and puff-balls popped up and the new grass started before Christmas.

But this year Christmas was not the central day to Jody. Some undetermined time in January had become the axis day around which the months swung. When the rains fell, he put Nellie in a box stall and fed her warm food every morning and curried her and brushed her.

The mare was swelling so greatly that Jody became alarmed. "She'll pop wide open," he said to Billy.

Billy laid his strong square hand against Nellie's swollen abdomen. "Feel here," he said quietly. "You can feel it move. I guess it would surprise you if there were twin colts."

"You don't think so?" Jody cried. "You don't think it will be twins, do you, Billy?"

"No, I don't, but it does happen, sometimes."

During the first two weeks of January it rained steadily. Jody spent most of his time, when he wasn't in school, in the box stall with Nellie. Twenty times a day he put his hand on her stomach to feel the colt move. Nellie became more and more gentle and friendly to him. She rubbed her nose on him. She whinnied softly when he walked into the barn.

Carl Tiflin came to the barn with Jody one day. He looked admiringly at the groomed bay coat, and he felt the firm flesh over ribs and shoulders. "You've done a good job," he said to Jody. And this was the greatest praise he knew how to give. Jody was tight with pride for hours afterward.

The fifteenth of January came, and the colt was not born. And the twentieth came; a lump of fear began to form in Jody's stomach. "Is it all right?" he demanded of Billy.

"Oh, sure."

And again, "Are you sure it's going to be all right?"

Billy stroked the mare's neck. She swayed her head uneasily. "I told you it wasn't always the same time, Jody. You just have to wait."

When the end of the month arrived with no birth, Jody grew frantic. Nellie was so big that her breath came heavily, and her ears were close together and straight up, as though her head ached. Jody's sleep grew restless, and his dreams confused.

On the night of the second of February he awakened crying. His mother called to him, "Jody, you're dreaming. Wake up and start over again."

But Jody was filled with terror and desolation. He lay quietly a few moments, waiting for his mother to go back to sleep, and then he slipped his clothes on, and crept out in his bare feet.

The night was black and thick. A little misting rain fell. The cypress tree and the bunkhouse loomed and then dropped back into the mist. The barn door screeched as he opened it, a thing it never did in the daytime. Jody went to the rack and found a lantern and a tin box of matches.

He lighted the wick and walked down the long straw-covered aisle to Nellie's stall. She was standing up. Her whole body weaved from side to side. Jody called to her, "So, Nellie, so-o, Nellie," but she did not stop her swaying nor look around. When he stepped into the stall and touched her on the shoulder she shivered under his hand. Then Billy Buck's voice came from the hayloft right above the stall.

"Jody, what are you doing?"

Jody started back and turned miserable eyes up toward the nest where Billy was lying in the hay. "Is she all right, do you think?"

"Why sure, I think so."

"You won't let anything happen, Billy, you're sure you won't?"

Billy growled down at him, "I told you I'd call you, and I will. Now you get back to bed and stop worrying that mare. She's got enough to do without you worrying her."

Jody cringed, for he had never heard Billy speak in such a tone. "I only thought I'd come and see," he said. "I woke up."

Billy softened a little then. "Well, you get to bed. I don't want you bothering her. I told you I'd get you a good colt. Get along now."

Jody walked slowly out of the barn. He blew out the lantern and set it in the rack. The blackness of the night, and the chilled mist struck him and enfolded him. He wished he believed everything Billy said as he had before the pony died. It was a moment before his eyes, blinded by the feeble lantern-flame, could make any form of the darkness. The damp ground chilled his bare feet. At the cypress tree the roosting turkeys chattered a little in alarm, and the two good dogs responded to their duty and came charging out, barking to frighten away the coyotes they thought were prowling under the tree.

As he crept through the kitchen, Jody stumbled over a

chair. Carl called from his bedroom, "Who's there? What's the matter there?"

And Mrs. Tiflin said sleepily, "What's the matter, Carl?"

The next second Carl came out of the bedroom carrying a candle, and found Jody before he could get into bed. "What are you doing out?"

Jody turned shyly away. "I was down to see the mare."

For a moment anger at being awakened fought with approval in Jody's father. "Listen," he said, finally, "there's not a man in this country that knows more about colts than Billy. You leave it to him."

Words burst out of Jody's mouth. "But the pony died ——"

"Don't you go blaming that on him," Carl said sternly. "If Billy can't save a horse, it can't be saved."

Mrs. Tiflin called, "Make him clean his feet and go to bed, Carl. He'll be sleepy all day tomorrow."

It seemed to Jody that he had just closed his eyes to try to go to sleep when he was shaken violently by the shoulder. Billy Buck stood beside him, holding a lantern in his hand. "Get up," he said. "Hurry up." He turned and walked quickly out of the room.

Mrs. Tiflin called, "What's the matter? Is that you, Billy?"

"Yes, ma'am."

"Is Nellie ready?"

"Yes, ma'am."

"All right, I'll get up and heat some water in case you need it."

Jody jumped into his clothes so quickly that he was out the back door before Billy's swinging lantern was halfway to the barn. There was a rim of dawn on the mountain-tops, but no light had penetrated into the cup of the ranch yet. Jody ran frantically after the lantern and caught up to Billy just as he reached the barn. Billy hung the lantern to a nail on the stallside and took off his blue denim coat. Jody saw that he wore only a sleeveless shirt under it.

Nellie was standing rigid and stiff. While they watched, she crouched. Her whole body was wrung with a spasm. The spasm passed. But in a few moments it started over again, and passed.

Billy muttered nervously, "There's something wrong." His bare hand disappeared. "Oh, Jesus," he said. "It's wrong."

The spasm came again, and this time Billy strained, and the muscles stood out on his arm and shoulder. He heaved strongly, his forehead beaded with perspiration. Nellie cried with pain. Billy was muttering, "It's wrong. I can't turn it. It's way wrong. It's turned all around wrong."

He glared wildly toward Jody. And then his fingers made a careful, careful diagnosis. His cheeks were growing tight and gray. He looked for a long questioning minute at Jody standing back of the stall. Then Billy stepped to the rack under the manure window and picked up a horseshoe hammer with his wet right hand.

"Go outside, Jody," he said.

The boy stood still and stared dully at him.

"Go outside, I tell you. It'll be too late."

Jody didn't move.

Then Billy walked quickly to Nellie's head. He cried, "Turn your face away, damn you, turn your face."

This time Jody obeyed. His head turned sideways. He heard Billy whispering hoarsely in the stall. And then he heard a hollow crunch of bone. Nellie chuckled shrilly. Jody looked back in time to see the hammer rise and fall again on the flat forehead. Then Nellie fell heavily to her side and quivered for a moment.

Billy jumped to the swollen stomach; his big pocket-knife was in his hand. He lifted the skin and drove the knife in. He sawed and ripped at the tough belly. The air filled with the sick odor of warm living entrails. The other horses reared back against their halter chains and squealed and kicked.

Billy dropped the knife. Both of his arms plunged into the terrible ragged hole and dragged out a big, white, dripping bundle. His teeth tore a hole in the covering. A little black head appeared through the tear, and little slick, wet ears. A gurgling breath was drawn, and then another. Billy shucked off the sac and found his knife and cut the string. For a moment he held the little black colt in his arms and looked at it. And then he walked slowly over and laid it in the straw at Jody's feet.

Billy's face and arms and chest were dripping red. His body shivered and his teeth chattered. His voice was gone; he spoke in a throaty whisper. "There's your colt. I promised. And there it is. I had to do it—had to." He stopped and looked over his shoulder into the box stall. "Go get hot water and a sponge," he whispered. "Wash him and dry him the way his mother would. You'll have to feed him by hand. But there's your colt, the way I promised."

Jody stared stupidly at the wet, panting foal. It stretched out its chin and tried to raise its head. Its blank eyes were navy blue.

"God damn you," Billy shouted, "will you go now for the water? *Will you go?*"

Then Jody turned and trotted out of the barn into the dawn. He ached from his throat to his stomach. His legs were stiff and heavy. He tried to be glad because of the colt, but the bloody face, and the haunted, tired eyes of Billy Buck hung in the air ahead of him.

4. The Leader of the People

ON Saturday afternoon Billy Buck, the ranch-hand, raked together the last of the old year's haystack and pitched small forkfuls over the wire fence to a few mildly interested cattle. High in the air small clouds like puffs of cannon smoke were driven eastward by the March wind. The wind could be heard whishing in the brush on the ridge crests, but no breath of it penetrated down into the ranch-cup.

The little boy, Jody, emerged from the house eating a thick piece of buttered bread. He saw Billy working on the last of the haystack. Jody tramped down scuffling his shoes in a way he had been told was destructive to good shoe-leather. A flock of white pigeons flew out of the black cypress tree as Jody passed, and circled the tree and landed again. A half-grown tortoise-shell cat leaped from the bunkhouse porch, galloped on stiff legs across the road, whirled and galloped back again. Jody picked up a stone to help the game along, but he was too late, for the cat was under the porch before the stone could be discharged. He threw the stone into the cypress tree and started the white pigeons on another whirling flight.

Arriving at the used-up haystack, the boy leaned against the barbed-wire fence. "Will that be all of it, do you think?" he asked.

The middle-aged ranch-hand stopped his careful raking and stuck his fork into the ground. He took off his black hat and smoothed down his hair. "Nothing left of it that isn't soggy from ground moisture," he said. He replaced his hat and rubbed his dry leathery hands together.

"Ought to be plenty mice," Jody suggested.

"Lousy with them," said Billy. "Just crawling with mice."

"Well, maybe, when you get all through, I could call the dogs and hunt the mice."

"Sure, I guess you could," said Billy Buck. He lifted a forkful of the damp ground-hay and threw it into the air. Instantly three mice leaped out and burrowed frantically under the hay again.

Jody sighed with satisfaction. Those plump, sleek, arrogant mice were doomed. For eight months they had lived and multiplied in the haystack. They had been immune from cats, from traps, from poison and from Jody. They had grown smug in their security, overbearing and fat. Now the time of disaster had come; they would not survive another day.

Billy looked up at the top of the hills that surrounded the ranch. "Maybe you better ask your father before you do it," he suggested.

"Well, where is he? I'll ask him now."

"He rode up to the ridge ranch after dinner. He'll be back pretty soon."

Jody slumped against the fence post. "I don't think he'd care."

As Billy went back to his work he said ominously, "You'd better ask him anyway. You know how he is."

Jody did know. His father, Carl Tiflin, insisted upon giving permission for anything that was done on the ranch, whether it was important or not. Jody sagged farther against the post until he was sitting on the ground. He looked up at the little puffs of wind-driven cloud. "Is it like to rain, Billy?"

"It might. The wind's good for it, but not strong enough."

"Well, I hope it don't rain until after I kill those damn mice." He looked over his shoulder to see whether Billy had noticed the mature profanity. Billy worked on without comment.

Jody turned back and looked at the side-hill where the road from the outside world came down. The hill was washed with lean March sunshine. Silver thistles, blue lupins and a few poppies bloomed among the sagebushes. Halfway up the hill Jody could see Doubletree Mutt, the black dog, digging in a squirrel hole. He paddled for a while and then paused to kick bursts of dirt out between his hind legs, and he dug with an earnestness which belied the knowledge he must have had that no dog had ever caught a squirrel by digging in a hole.

Suddenly, while Jody watched, the black dog stiffened, and backed out of the hole and looked up the hill toward the cleft in the ridge where the road came through. Jody looked up too. For a moment Carl Tiflin on horseback stood out against the pale sky and then he moved down the road toward the house. He carried something white in his hand.

The boy started to his feet. "He's got a letter," Jody cried. He trotted away toward the ranch house, for the letter would probably be read aloud and he wanted to be there. He reached the house before his father did, and ran in. He heard Carl dismount from his creaking saddle and slap the horse on the side to send it to the barn where Billy would unsaddle it and turn it out.

Jody ran into the kitchen. "We got a letter!" he cried.

His mother looked up from a pan of beans. "Who has?"

"Father has. I saw it in his hand."

Carl strode into the kitchen then, and Jody's mother asked, "Who's the letter from, Carl?"

He frowned quickly. "How did you know there was a letter?"

She nodded her head in the boy's direction. "Big-Britches Jody told me."

Jody was embarrassed.

His father looked down at him contemptuously. "He *is* getting to be a Big-Britches," Carl said. "He's minding everybody's business but his own. Got his big nose into everything."

Mrs. Tiflin relented a little. "Well, he hasn't enough to keep him busy. Who's the letter from?"

Carl still frowned on Jody. "I'll keep him busy if he isn't careful." He held out a sealed letter. "I guess it's from your father."

Mrs. Tiflin took a hairpin from her head and slit open the flap. Her lips pursed judiciously. Jody saw her eyes snap back and forth over the lines. "He says," she translated, "he says he's going to drive out Saturday to stay for a little while. Why, this is Saturday. The letter must have been delayed." She looked at the postmark. "This was mailed day before yesterday. It should have been here yesterday." She looked up questioningly at her husband, and then her face darkened angrily. "Now what have you got that look on you for? He doesn't come often."

Carl turned his eyes away from her anger. He could be stern with her most of the time, but when occasionally her temper arose, he could not combat it.

"What's the matter with you?" she demanded again.

In his explanation there was a tone of apology Jody himself might have used. "It's just that he talks," Carl said lamely. "Just talks."

"Well, what of it? You talk yourself."

"Sure I do. But your father only talks about one thing."

"Indians!" Jody broke in excitedly. "Indians and crossing the plains!"

Carl turned fiercely on him. "You get out, Mr. Big-Britches! Go on, now! Get out!"

Jody went miserably out the back door and closed the screen with elaborate quietness. Under the kitchen window his shamed, downcast eyes fell upon a curiously shaped stone, a stone of such fascination that he squatted down and picked it up and turned it over in his hands.

The voices came clearly to him through the open kitchen window. "Jody's damn well right," he heard his father say. "Just Indians and crossing the plains. I've heard that story about how the horses got driven off about a thousand times. He just goes on and on, and he never changes a word in the things he tells."

When Mrs. Tiflin answered her tone was so changed that Jody, outside the window, looked up from his study of the stone. Her voice had become soft and explanatory. Jody knew how her face would have changed to match the tone. She said quietly, "Look at it this way, Carl. That was the big thing in my father's life. He led a wagon train clear across the plains to the coast, and when it was finished, his life was done. It was a big thing to do, but it didn't last long enough. Look!" she continued, "it's as though he was born to do that, and after he finished it, there wasn't anything more for him to do but think about it and talk about it. If there'd been any farther west to go, he'd have gone. He's told me so himself. But at last there was the ocean. He lives right by the ocean where he had to stop."

She had caught Carl, caught him and entangled him in her soft tone.

"I've seen him," he agreed quietly. "He goes down and stares off west over the ocean." His voice sharpened a little. "And then he goes up to the Horseshoe Club in Pacific Grove, and he tells people how the Indians drove off the horses."

She tried to catch him again. "Well, it's everything to him. You might be patient with him and pretend to listen."

Carl turned impatiently away. "Well, if it gets too bad, I can always go down to the bunkhouse and sit with Billy," he said irritably. He walked through the house and slammed the front door after him.

Jody ran to his chores. He dumped the grain to the chickens without chasing any of them. He gathered the eggs from the nests. He trotted into the house with the wood and interlaced it so carefully in the wood-box that two armloads seemed to fill it to overflowing.

His mother had finished the beans by now. She stirred up the fire and brushed off the stove-top with a turkey wing. Jody peered cautiously at her to see whether any rancor toward him remained. "Is he coming today?" Jody asked.

"That's what his letter said."

"Maybe I better walk up the road to meet him."

Mrs. Tiflin clanged the stove-lid shut. "That would be nice," she said. "He'd probably like to be met."

"I guess I'll just do it then."

Outside, Jody whistled shrilly to the dogs. "Come on up the hill," he commanded. The two dogs waved their tails and ran ahead. Along the roadside the sage had tender new tips. Jody tore off some pieces and rubbed them on his hands until the air was filled with the sharp wild smell. With a rush the dogs leaped from the road and yapped into the brush after a rabbit. That was the last Jody saw of them, for when they failed to catch the rabbit, they went back home.

Jody plodded on up the hill toward the ridge top. When he reached the little cleft where the road came through, the afternoon wind struck him and blew up his hair and ruffled his shirt. He looked down on the little hills and ridges below and then out at the huge green Salinas Valley. He could see the white town of Salinas far out in the flat and the flash of its windows under the waning sun. Directly below him, in an oak tree, a crow congress had convened. The tree was black with crows all cawing at once. Then Jody's eyes followed the wagon road down from the ridge where he stood, and lost it behind a hill, and picked it up again on the other side. On that distant stretch he saw a cart slowly pulled by a bay horse. It disappeared behind the hill. Jody sat down on the ground and watched the place where the cart would reappear again. The wind sang on the hilltops and the puff-ball clouds hurried eastward.

Then the cart came into sight and stopped. A man dressed in black dismounted from the seat and walked to the horse's head. Although it was so far away, Jody knew he had unhooked the check-rein, for the horse's head dropped forward. The horse moved on, and the man walked slowly up the hill beside it. Jody gave a glad cry and ran down the road toward them. The squirrels bumped along off the road, and a road-runner flirted its tail and raced over the edge of the hill and sailed out like a glider.

Jody tried to leap into the middle of his shadow at every step. A stone rolled under his foot and he went down.

Around a little bend he raced, and there, a short distance ahead, were his grandfather and the cart. The boy dropped from his unseemly running and approached at a dignified walk.

The horse plodded stumble-footedly up the hill and the old man walked beside it. In the lowering sun their giant shadows flickered darkly behind them. The grandfather was dressed in a black broadcloth suit and he wore kid congress gaiters and a black tie on a short, hard collar. He carried his black slouch hat in his hand. His white beard was cropped close and his white eyebrows overhung his eyes like mustaches. The blue eyes were sternly merry. About the whole face and figure there was a granite dignity, so that every motion seemed an impossible thing. Once at rest, it seemed the old man would be stone, would never move again. His steps were slow and certain. Once made, no step could ever be retraced; once headed in a direction, the path would never bend nor the pace increase nor slow.

When Jody appeared around the bend, Grandfather waved his hat slowly in welcome, and he called, "Why, Jody! Come down to meet me, have you?"

Jody sidled near and turned and matched his step to the old man's step and stiffened his body and dragged his heels a little. "Yes, sir," he said. "We got your letter only today."

"Should have been here yesterday," said Grandfather. "It certainly should. How are all the folks?"

"They're fine, sir." He hesitated and then suggested shyly, "Would you like to come on a mouse hunt tomorrow, sir?"

"Mouse hunt, Jody?" Grandfather chuckled. "Have the people of this generation come down to hunting mice? They aren't very strong, the new people, but I hardly thought mice would be game for them."

"No, sir. It's just play. The haystack's gone. I'm going to

drive out the mice to the dogs. And you can watch, or even beat the hay a little."

The stern, merry eyes turned down on him. "I see. You don't eat them, then. You haven't come to that yet."

Jody explained, "The dogs eat them, sir. It wouldn't be much like hunting Indians, I guess."

"No, not much—but then later, when the troops were hunting Indians and shooting children and burning teepees, it wasn't much different from your mouse hunt."

They topped the rise and started down into the ranch-cup, and they lost the sun from their shoulders. "You've grown," Grandfather said. "Nearly an inch, I should say."

"More," Jody boasted. "Where they mark me on the door, I'm up more than an inch since Thanksgiving even."

Grandfather's rich throaty voice said, "Maybe you're getting too much water and turning to pith and stalk. Wait until you head out, and then we'll see."

Jody looked quickly into the old man's face to see whether his feelings should be hurt, but there was no will to injure, no punishing nor putting-in-your-place light in the keen blue eyes. "We might kill a pig," Jody suggested.

"Oh, no! I couldn't let you do that. You're just humoring me. It isn't the time and you know it."

"You know Riley, the big boar, sir?"

"Yes. I remember Riley well."

"Well, Riley ate a hole into that same haystack, and it fell down on him and smothered him."

"Pigs do that when they can," said Grandfather.

"Riley was a nice pig, for a boar, sir. I rode him sometimes, and he didn't mind."

A door slammed at the house below them, and they saw Jody's mother standing on the porch waving her apron in welcome. And they saw Carl Tiflin walking up from the barn to be at the house for the arrival.

The sun had disappeared from the hills by now. The blue smoke from the house chimney hung in flat layers in the purpling ranch-cup. The puff-ball clouds, dropped by the falling wind, hung listlessly in the sky.

Billy Buck came out of the bunkhouse and flung a wash-basin of soapy water on the ground. He had been shaving in midweek, for Billy held Grandfather in reverence, and Grandfather said that Billy was one of the few men of the new generation who had not gone soft. Although Billy was in middle age, Grandfather considered him a boy. Now Billy was hurrying toward the house too.

When Jody and Grandfather arrived, the three were waiting for them in front of the yard gate.

Carl said, "Hello, sir. We've been looking for you."

Mrs. Tiflin kissed Grandfather on the side of his beard, and stood still while his big hand patted her shoulder. Billy shook hands solemnly, grinning under his straw mustache. "I'll put up your horse," said Billy, and he led the rig away.

Grandfather watched him go, and then, turning back to the group, he said as he had said a hundred times before, "There's a good boy. I knew his father, old Mule-tail Buck. I never knew why they called him Mule-tail except he packed mules."

Mrs. Tiflin turned and led the way into the house. "How long are you going to stay, Father? Your letter didn't say."

"Well, I don't know. I thought I'd stay about two weeks. But I never stay as long as I think I'm going to."

In a short while they were sitting at the white oilcloth table eating their supper. The lamp with the tin reflector hung over the table. Outside the dining-room windows the big moths battered softly against the glass.

Grandfather cut his steak into tiny pieces and chewed slowly. "I'm hungry," he said. "Driving out here got my appetite up. It's like when we were crossing. We all got so hungry every night we could hardly wait to let the meat get done. I could eat about five pounds of buffalo meat every night."

"It's moving around does it," said Billy. "My father was a government packer. I helped him when I was a kid. Just the two of us could about clean up a deer's ham."

"I knew your father, Billy," said Grandfather. "A fine man he was. They called him Mule-tail Buck. I don't know why except he packed mules."

"That was it," Billy agreed. "He packed mules."

Grandfather put down his knife and fork and looked around the table. "I remember one time we ran out of meat —" His voice dropped to a curious low sing-song, dropped into a tonal groove the story had worn for itself. "There was no buffalo, no antelope, not even rabbits. The hunters couldn't even shoot a coyote. That was the time for the leader to be on the watch. I was the leader, and I kept my eyes open. Know why? Well, just the minute the people began to get hungry they'd start slaughtering the team oxen. Do you believe that? I've heard of parties that just ate up their draft cattle. Started from the middle and worked toward the ends. Finally they'd eat the lead pair, and then the wheelers. The leader of a party had to keep them from doing that."

In some manner a big moth got into the room and circled the hanging kerosene lamp. Billy got up and tried to clap it between his hands. Carl struck with a cupped palm and caught the moth and broke it. He walked to the window and dropped it out.

"As I was saying," Grandfather began again, but Carl interrupted him. "You'd better eat some more meat. All the rest of us are ready for our pudding."

Jody saw a flash of anger in his mother's eyes. Grandfather picked up his knife and fork. "I'm pretty hungry, all right," he said. "I'll tell you about that later."

When supper was over, when the family and Billy Buck sat in front of the fireplace in the other room, Jody anxiously watched Grandfather. He saw the signs he knew. The bearded head leaned forward; the eyes lost their sternness and looked wonderingly into the fire; the big lean fingers laced themselves on the black knees.

"I wonder," he began, "I just wonder whether I ever told you how those thieving Piutes drove off thirty-five of our horses."

"I think you did," Carl interrupted. "Wasn't it just before you went up into the Tahoe country?"

Grandfather turned quickly toward his son-in-law. "That's right. I guess I must have told you that story."

"Lots of times," Carl said cruelly, and he avoided his wife's eyes. But he felt the angry eyes on him, and he said, " 'Course I'd like to hear it again."

Grandfather looked back at the fire. His fingers unlaced and laced again. Jody knew how he felt, how his insides were collapsed and empty. Hadn't Jody been called a Big-Britches that very afternoon? He arose to heroism and opened himself to the term Big-Britches again. "Tell about Indians," he said softly.

Grandfather's eyes grew stern again. "Boys always want to hear about Indians. It was a job for men, but boys want to hear about it. Well, let's see. Did I ever tell you how I wanted each wagon to carry a long iron plate?"

Everyone but Jody remained silent. Jody said, "No. You didn't."

"Well, when the Indians attacked, we always put the wagons in a circle and fought from between the wheels. I thought that if every wagon carried a long plate with rifle holes, the men could stand the plates on the outside of the wheels when the wagons were in the circle and they would be protected. It would save lives and that would make up for the extra weight of the iron. But of course the party wouldn't do it. No party had done it before and they couldn't see why they should go to the expense. They lived to regret it, too."

Jody looked at his mother, and knew from her expression that she was not listening at all. Carl picked at a callus on his thumb and Billy Buck watched a spider crawling up the wall.

Grandfather's tone dropped into its narrative groove again. Jody knew in advance exactly what words would fall. The story droned on, speeded up for the attack, grew sad over the wounds, struck a dirge at the burials on the great plains. Jody sat quietly watching Grandfather. The stern blue eyes were detached. He looked as though he were not very interested in the story himself.

When it was finished, when the pause had been politely respected as the frontier of the story, Billy Buck stood up and stretched and hitched his trousers. "I guess I'll turn in," he said. Then he faced Grandfather. "I've got an old powder horn and a cap and ball pistol down to the bunkhouse. Did I ever show them to you?"

Grandfather nodded slowly. "Yes, I think you did, Billy. Reminds me of a pistol I had when I was leading the people across." Billy stood politely until the little story was done, and then he said, "Good night," and went out of the house.

Carl Tiflin tried to turn the conversation then. "How's the country between here and Monterey? I've heard it's pretty dry."

"It is dry," said Grandfather. "There's not a drop of water in the Laguna Seca. But it's a long pull from '87. The whole country was powder then, and in '61 I believe all the coyotes starved to death. We had fifteen inches of rain this year."

"Yes, but it all came too early. We could do with some now." Carl's eye fell on Jody. "Hadn't you better be getting to bed?"

Jody stood up obediently. "Can I kill the mice in the old haystack, sir?"

"Mice? Oh! Sure, kill them all off. Billy said there isn't any good hay left."

Jody exchanged a secret and satisfying look with Grandfather. "I'll kill every one tomorrow," he promised.

Jody lay in his bed and thought of the impossible world of Indians and buffaloes, a world that had ceased to be forever. He wished he could have been living in the heroic time, but he knew he was not of heroic timber. No one living now, save possibly Billy Buck, was worthy to do the things that had been done. A race of giants had lived then, fearless men, men of a staunchness unknown in this day. Jody thought of the wide plains and of the wagons moving across like centipedes. He thought of Grandfather on a huge white horse, marshaling the people. Across his mind marched the great phantoms, and they marched off the earth and they were gone.

He came back to the ranch for a moment, then. He heard the dull rushing sound that space and silence make. He heard one of the dogs, out in the doghouse, scratching a flea and bumping his elbow against the floor with every stroke. Then the wind arose again and the black cypress groaned and Jody went to sleep.

He was up half an hour before the triangle sounded for breakfast. His mother was rattling the stove to make the flames roar when Jody went through the kitchen. "You're up early," she said. "Where are you going?"

"Out to get a good stick. We're going to kill the mice today."

"Who is 'we'?"

"Why, Grandfather and I."

"So you've got him in it. You always like to have some one in with you in case there's blame to share."

"I'll be right back," said Jody. "I just want to have a good stick ready for after breakfast.

He closed the screen door after him and went out into the cool blue morning. The birds were noisy in the dawn and the ranch cats came down from the hill like blunt snakes. They had been hunting gophers in the dark, and although the four cats were full of gopher meat, they sat in a semi-circle at the back door and mewed piteously for milk. Doubletree Mutt and Smasher moved sniffing along the edge of the brush, performing the duty with rigid ceremony, but when Jody whistled, their heads jerked up and their tails waved. They plunged down to him, wriggling their skins and yawning. Jody patted their heads seriously, and moved on to the weathered scrap pile. He selected an old broom handle and a short piece of inch-square scrap wood. From his pocket he took a shoelace and tied the ends of the sticks loosly together to make a flail. He whistled his new weapon through the air and struck the ground experimentally, while the dogs leaped aside and whined with apprehension.

Jody turned and started down past the house toward the old haystack ground to look over the field of slaughter, but Billy Buck, sitting patiently on the back steps, called to him, "You better come back. It's only a couple of minutes till breakfast."

Jody changed his course and moved toward the house. He leaned his flail against the steps. "That's to drive the mice out," he said. "I'll bet they're fat. I'll bet they don't know what's going to happen to them today."

"No, nor you either," Billy remarked philosophically, "nor me, nor anyone."

Jody was staggered by this thought. He knew it was true. His imagination twitched away from the mouse hunt. Then his mother came out on the back porch and struck the triangle, and all thoughts fell in a heap.

Grandfather hadn't appeared at the table when they sat

down. Billy nodded at his empty chair. "He's all right? He isn't sick?"

"He takes a long time to dress," said Mrs. Tiflin. "He combs his whiskers and rubs up his shoes and brushes his clothes."

Carl scattered sugar on his mush. "A man that's led a wagon train across the plains has got to be pretty careful how he dresses."

Mrs. Tiflin turned on him. "Don't do that, Carl! Please don't!" There was more of threat than of request in her tone. And the threat irritated Carl.

"Well, how many times do I have to listen to the story of the iron plates, and the thirty-five horses? That time's done. Why can't he forget it, now it's done?" He grew angrier while he talked, and his voice rose. "Why does he have to tell them over and over? He came across the plains. All right! Now it's finished. Nobody wants to hear about it over and over."

The door into the kitchen closed softly. The four at the table sat frozen. Carl laid his mush spoon on the table and touched his chin with his fingers.

Then the kitchen door opened and Grandfather walked in. His mouth smiled tightly and his eyes were squinted. "Good morning," he said, and he sat down and looked at his mush dish.

Carl could not leave it there. "Did-did you hear what I said?"

Grandfather jerked a little nod.

"I don't know what got into me, sir. I didn't mean it. I was just being funny."

Jody glanced in shame at his mother, and he saw that she was looking at Carl, and that she wasn't breathing. It was an awful thing that he was doing. He was tearing himself to pieces to talk like that. It was a terrible thing to him to retract a word, but to retract it in shame was infinitely worse.

Grandfather looked sidewise. "I'm trying to get right side up," he said gently. "I'm not being mad. I don't mind what you said, but it might be true, and I would mind that."

"It isn't true," said Carl. "I'm not feeling well this morning. I'm sorry I said it."

"Don't be sorry, Carl. An old man doesn't see things sometimes. Maybe you're right. The crossing is finished. Maybe it should be forgotten, now it's done."

Carl got up from the table. "I've had enough to eat. I'm going to work. Take your time, Billy!" He walked quickly out of the dining-room. Billy gulped the rest of his food and followed soon after. But Jody could not leave his chair.

"Won't you tell any more stories?" Jody asked.

"Why, sure I'll tell them, but only when—I'm sure people want to hear them."

"I like to hear them, sir."

"Oh! Of course you do, but you're a little boy. It was a job for men, but only little boys like to hear about it."

Jody got up from his place. "I'll wait outside for you, sir. I've got a good stick for those mice."

He waited by the gate until the old man came out on the porch. "Let's go down and kill the mice now," Jody called.

"I think I'll just sit in the sun, Jody. You go kill the mice."

"You can use my stick if you like."

"No, I'll just sit here a while."

Jody turned disconsolately away, and walked down toward the old haystack. He tried to whip up his enthusiasm with thoughts of the fat juicy mice. He beat the ground with his flail. The dogs coaxed and whined about him, but he could not go. Back at the house he could see Grandfather sitting on the porch, looking small and thin and black.

Jody gave up and went to sit on the steps at the old man's feet.

"Back already? Did you kill the mice?"

"No, sir. I'll kill them some other day."

The morning flies buzzed close to the ground and the ants dashed about in front of the steps. The heavy smell of sage slipped down the hill. The porch boards grew warm in the sunshine.

Jody hardly knew when Grandfather started to talk. "I shouldn't stay here, feeling the way I do." He examined his strong old hands. "I feel as though the crossing wasn't worth doing." His eyes moved up the side-hill and stopped on a motionless hawk perched on a dead limb. "I tell those old stories, but they're not what I want to tell. I only know how I want people to feel when I tell them.

"It wasn't Indians that were important, nor adventures, nor even getting out here. It was a whole bunch of people made into one big crawling beast. And I was the head. It was westering and westering. Every man wanted something for himself, but the big beast that was all of them wanted only westering. I was the leader, but if I hadn't been there, someone else would have been the head. The thing had to have a head.

"Under the little bushes the shadows were black at white noonday. When we saw the mountains at last, we cried—all of us. But it wasn't getting here that mattered, it was movement and westering.

"We carried life out here and set it down the way those ants carry eggs. And I was the leader. The westering was as big as God, and the slow steps that made the movement piled up and piled up until the continent was crossed.

"Then we came down to the sea, and it was done." He stopped and wiped his eyes until the rims were red. "That's what I should be telling instead of stories."

When Jody spoke, Grandfather stared and looked down at him. "Maybe I could lead the people some day," Jody said.

The old man smiled. "There's no place to go. There's the

ocean to stop you. There's a line of old men along the shore hating the ocean because it stopped them."

"In boats I might, sir."

"No place to go, Jody. Every place is taken. But that's not the worst—no, not the worst. Westering has died out of the people. Westering isn't a hunger any more. It's all done. Your father is right. It is finished." He laced his fingers on his knee and looked at them.

Jody felt very sad. "If you'd like a glass of lemonade I could make it for you."

Grandfather was about to refuse, and then he saw Jody's face. "That would be nice," he said. "Yes, it would be nice to drink a lemonade."

Jody ran into the kitchen where his mother was wiping the last of the breakfast dishes. "Can I have a lemon to make a lemonade for Grandfather?"

His mother mimicked—"And another lemon to make a lemonade for you."

"No, ma'am. I don't want one."

"Jody! You're sick!" Then she stopped suddenly. "Take a lemon out of the cooler," she said softly. "Here, I'll reach the squeezer down to you."

A selection of books published by Penguin is listed on the following page. For a complete list of books available from Penguin in the United States, write to Dept. DG, Penguin Books, 299 Murray Hill Parkway, East Rutherford, New Jersey 07073.

In Canada for a complete list of Penguin Books write to Penguin Books Canada Limited, 2801 John Street, Markham, Ontario L3R 1B4.

John Steinbeck

THE GRAPES OF WRATH

This famous novel about the Joad family's migration from Oklahoma to California in search of work represents the plight of all dispossessed people everywhere. First published in 1939, it electrified an America still not recovered from the depression. Alexander Woollcott called it "as great a book as has yet come out of America," and Dorothy Parker said, "*The Grapes of Wrath* is the greatest American novel I have ever read." Today, because of the eloquent conviction that Steinbeck brought to the writing, it retains all its nobility and power.

THE LOG FROM THE *SEA OF CORTEZ*

In 1940 John Steinbeck and his friend the biologist Ed Ricketts ventured into the Gulf of California in search of marine invertebrates. Their expedition was described in *Sea of Cortez*, published in 1941. *The Log from the* Sea of Cortez, taken from the longer book, tells the exciting day-by-day story of the trip. Combining science, philosophy, and high-spirited adventure, it is unique in Steinbeck's work. As Lewis Gannett wrote: "This is at once the record of a serious biological expedition and of the impact of a biologist and a novelist upon each other's minds—a kind of human sociology. . . . The best of Steinbeck is in it—the mellowest and the crotchetiest."

THE PORTABLE STEINBECK
(Revised and Enlarged Edition)
Introduction, biographical and
bibliographical notes
by Pascal Covici, Jr.

Includes *Of Mice and Men* complete, short stories, and selections from *Tortilla Flat, In Dubious Battle, Cannery Row,* and others.